CORE

OF

CONFLICTION

BY

MAQUEL A. JACOB

Published by
MAJart Works
2001 NW Aloclek Dr Suite 211
Hillsboro, Oregon 97124
http://www.majartworks.com

Cover Art by Dar Albert
www.wickedsmartdesigns.com

Books by

MAQUEL A. JACOB

THE CORE TRILOGY

SEEDS OF CONVICTION

BONDS OF CONTRITION

WELCOME DESPAIR

A COLLECTION OF SHORTS

CURVE OF HUMANITY

ORIGINS
SHADOWMEN OBJECTIVE
PURGE SEQUENCE
CRIPPLED EARTH

THE BLOOD SAGA

BLOOD DOCTRINE

BLOOD DOMINION

ACKNOWLEDGEMENTS

A huge thanks to NaNoWriMo (National Novel Writing Month) for having a platform to support writers' creative juices. Without them I would not have pushed myself or met Dr. Laurel Standley who helped keep me on track and contributed in more ways than I can express.

NIWA (Northwest Independent Writers Association) thank you for letting me in your organization and wave my flag at so many book signing opportunities. I am truly grateful to all the fellow authors I met.

For all of my friends, family and classmates, the wait is over. It took a little over two decades, but better late than never. To my early stage beta readers: my sincere condolences and immense gratitude. Big thanks to Chris Downing for helping me come up with the title.

To Sarah Walker, Robert "Fuzzy" Baker, Greg Hallock, Kamila Miller, and Mom for all the honest feedback and encouraging my passion.

ONE:

What on Earth

Charles hated strip malls.

The socially tainted badlands of suburban America that spread like a virus through small towns and barren areas in need of construction. They were like a ghost town during working hours, somehow maintaining business with the help of weekend warriors. It was a mystery how those infestations came about. Something to do with revenue. Every one of them developed out of the machine, in cookie cutter fashion, tailored to the demographics of its proposed district.

This particular one set the bar a little lower. Indigenous trees, held upright by two sticks and a chain hidden from view by their foliage, were planted strategically around the perimeter with benches nearby. A designated eating area, littered with ugly round umbrella topped tables, was right smack in the middle with long picnic style benches to sit at on either side of them. Cigarette butts were scattered on the ground and there was no telling what lay directly under the table tops.

His own justification for being there; it was the only place within close proximity of his territory that had offerings of sustenance resembling something edible.

His team consisted of two other men and one woman. They sat at one of the eatery benches with him waiting for their order of cheap pizzas. He used a coupon to get the buy three get one free special, so everyone could have their own.

They were taking a break from their daily drug runs and as long as his team met their dealer quota for the boss, nothing else mattered. Right now, it was not worth the wait.

Glancing up at the sky he watched the sun struggling to peek out from behind the clouds. Even without direct sunlight the heat lingered, prompting Sara to let out a heavy sigh.

"Aww, it's hot," she whined.

Having his reverie disturbed irritated not only him, but the other two men who turned towards her with disdain. This was an ongoing thing and today there was no reason to state the obvious. Charles felt like he was being steam ironed with his clothes on. They were all tired, hot, and hungry.

He watched Sara try to tame her unruly more- dirty -than - blonde curly hair, frizzing from the heat, with an old tattered hair tie. She looked sloppy and miserable as usual, sitting next to her dealing partner, Klein, who kept repeatedly pulling on his shirt to force some sort of breeze down into it. His thick brown mop of hair was retaining the heat and sweat dampened the sides of his face.

"Man! Give me airconditioning or death."

Charles was ready to give him the latter.

It didn't help matters that they were all dressed in their organization's so-called uniform of dark slacks and a grey polo shirt sporting its logo on the left sleeve. Not a summer outfit by any means. All it needed to be complete was a baseball cap and they would look like workers ready to do an armored truck heist. Having the organization's logo in plain sight helped society identify them as criminals. It was run by a new crime boss who came on the scene unknown and eliminated most of the competition.

Many from the old guard now operated under the organization's umbrella. There were factions of Yakuza, Russian Mafia and Triad members. The boss had no qualms of broadcasting his activities. On one hand, it made illegal deals a little difficult in heavily policed areas, and with competitors rolling through territories to shoot them on sight. The upside, not many people messed with them.

Their employer seemed to not take anything lightly, even the occasional legitimate arrest, care of local law enforcement. Bodies of innocent bystanders, federal agents and snitches were found in various forms of dismemberment within the city.

So much for discretion.

An older lady came out of the pizzeria and walked toward the courtyard. Her silver curly hair was tucked neatly under a baseball cap with an image of a pizza slice embroidered on the front. Her white shirt had the same design on the sleeves. She scooted merrily along, her posture perfect as she carried the large pizza in the palm of one hand. Although one could tell she was older, there was not a wrinkle on her face and her eyes had an unnatural spark in them.

To the group's disappointment, she made a beeline for the only other people in the area and delivered their order. As she turned to head back into the pizzeria, she acknowledged Charles with a wink and went through the glass doors of Rooter's Pizza Parlor. Another sigh from Sara was rewarded with yet another look of utter exasperation by the men.

"I'm starving." Sara literally pouted.

The youngest of the three men, Jared, reached down and petted his German Shepard, who lounged by his feet. His short dark hair and pale skin with androgynous facial features gave him an exotic, almost feminine, appeal. Being underweight for his five-foot eleven frame did not make it any better.

When Charles had first met him, he thought 'what a scrawny woman'. The dog yawned and settled further down on the ground. He too appeared to be tired, hot, and possibly hungry.

Charles turned his right wrist over to check his watch as he ran the other hand through his hair. It was short in the back and longer in the front, so when his gel-sculpting technique completely unraveled it flopped forward. He could tell, by the greasy feel on his fingers, the heat had evaporated any hair products that might have existed in it. There really was no point in grooming it in the summer-time. Despite knowing this, his vanity always kicked in at the last minute each morning. He understood it was not a popular trait, though it got him by. A stomach was heard growling and he looked around to see whose it was. No one gave the impression they were the culprit. Someone glanced at the dog.

The silver haired lady came back out with a stack of pizza boxes, heading their way. All of them came to attention in anticipation. Finally, sustenance had arrived and not a moment too soon. Any longer and they would be drooling shamelessly. She smiled wide, setting the load down on the edge of the table. Charles gave her a tip of ten dollars and thanked her graciously.

"You are a life saver. Thank you so much."

"Not a problem, dearie." Her voice sounded younger than her looks. She had barely left the bench when hands attacked the boxes, dragging them to each hungry team member.

While they ate in silence, he saw Klein notice some weird items laying on the ground near their bench. There was a knobby ball, some dice, some other small items he couldn't decipher and a wide tooth comb. None of these things were around the bench before the pizza came so it dawned on all of them, simultaneously, that the older woman must have dropped them there, which seemed odd, raising suspicion and heightened paranoia. Their organization had a running supply of enemies.

There was enough garbage laying around where they sat and less was better. Klein eyed her as she headed back to the pizzeria, seeing she had no intention of coming back. Instead of getting up to ask her if the items belong to her he leaned down to the left of him, scooped the items up in one hand and tossed them away towards the nearby trees. He nodded to himself in justification. Charles raise an eyebrow at him.

While the items were still in midair, the German Shepard leapt up and with one swipe of his paw, knocked them back to the ground. As he landed, all the items, except for the wide toothed comb secured in his mouth, lay scattered around him. He trotted back and to the group's amazement, climbed up onto the bench and sat down as if he were a person. Extending his left paw to remove the comb from his mouth he enclosed the comb in a fist.

No one else was around save the old lady who stopped halfway to the pizzeria to watch, and the customers sitting under one of the umbrella topped tables farthest from the store front. Charles's group leaned back in unison away from the dog as it combed its mane, each stroke further transforming it into a different creature.

The nose moved upward as the eyes set wider apart. Its limbs lengthened and grew meatier to compensate for the torso elongating. The fur became less dense, almost fine covering a beast now twice its original size. Strips of cloth whirled around it assembling into a garment of sorts.

Jared was seated next to the creature and his eyes started to glaze over while Sara and Klein sat dumbfounded across from him. The dog was now a six foot four-inch-tall wolf like creature wearing a Japanese style monks robe. Its mane was dark brown, cascading down its back with the top like a lion's, adding another three inches to its height.

"I always wear my hair like this," the wolf like creature spoke.

Silence. Not a word, a bird, or wind could be heard. Charles had not moved. The moment he blinked, all hell broke loose as Sara and Klein abandoned their pizzas to attack the creature.

Sara went low with a punch. It dodged her attempt as Klein hopped onto the top of the bench to deliver a flying kick. That too was a miss. Not assassin quality fighters by any means, they did learn a few things from various members of the organization. The two advanced, each trying to land a hit, the creature's reflexes just too fast for any to connect.

When the creature morphed again into a more human, less hairy, form its arms bulged with muscles and the mouth now resembled that of a lion. The massive frame grew wider, yet its reflexes sped up. Sara and Klein were able to get a quick nod to each other before going into a defense stance. There was a second of no movement.

Both parties launched at each other and a melee ensued. Sara was bobbing and weaving like a boxer to avoid getting hit to no avail. The creature's claws had got her a few times while she tried to match its speed, only grazing her. She never knew she could move that fast.

In her peripheral view to the left she could see Klein

using some of the martial arts techniques he learned from a triad member. He too moved faster than she had ever seen and not doing so well either. She came back to attention in time to see the claws swipe in front of her eyes as she leaned back almost in a back bend. Jumping back, she slid to a stop and launched herself back into the fight. Klein needed back up, fast.

Charles watched the combat with no expression on his face. They were moving so fast a normal person would only see blurred lines of color. He had seen such lightning fast fighting techniques from the organization's high level enforcers so his eyes were able to track each motion.

Enforcers were a strange breed of unarmed soldiers commanded by the top generals. Many of them did not quite resemble humans and their strength was unparalleled. When those enforcers were sent out, you were in trouble. Their fighting skills seemed other worldly with movements rivaling the speed of light and blows capable of caving in the side of buildings. The bear like creature moved just like them, Sara and Klein somehow keeping up. His mind calculated every movement.

Jared now sat in shock and great danger of getting hit by any one of the bodies moving at incredible speed around him, and he was oblivious to it all. The, now human like, creature saw his body sway and switched maneuvers in order to protect Jared from the chaos. He slowed down the speed of his attacks while still holding Sara and Klein at bay.

The older woman ran back to the area and stopped near the bench. She picked up the ball, which tuned into a glowing orb, and extended her hands out in front of her. It became a blackish blue vortex forming between them and as it grew, floated upwards then back to position itself behind her. Its gaping mouth gave view to the twinkling darkness of a universe swirling at dizzying speed.

Strong wind shot from it, making a weird sucking sound as it started to pull the man beast, Jared, and the older woman in. The man beast wrapped his arms around Jared, securing him tightly as they were sucked in, while the older lady dug her heels in the dry dirt to keep the vortex steady.

In a soft deep voice, the man beast tried to reassure a comatose Jared.

"Everything will be okay now, I promise. I will protect you always."

The vortex snapped shut like a vice once the older woman stepped inside it, leaving no trace of its existence or the people it consumed. In the blink of an eye, everything screeched to a halt. Sara and Klein stood poised for attack, breathing heavily, frozen in place. The center of the strip mall bore witness to scattered debris, two wild eyed men and a deranged looking female. Across the way, the other customers sat mid consumption of their pizza. Slices had fallen onto the table and the ground from their hands, now empty.

"What the fuck!" Sara screamed, breaking the silence.

That snapped them out of their shock. Grabbing their things, the other customers abandoned the pizza and ran to the parking lot.

Noticing he had tried not to breathe in quite a while, Charles took a few breaths then shook his head to clear it as he replayed the scene. He concluded, based on the fighting skills of the former German Shepard and the teleportation used by the older woman, they were a possible enemy of the organization and whatever that black hole was did not belong on Earth. He wondered how they knew his team was going to be there at this hour. It smacked of a set up leaving a bad taste in his mouth.

"You guys go on ahead and make a report. I am going to find out some more info since it's obvious we were targeted. There's a contact not far from here so, don't call me. I'll come talk to you guys later."

He stood and left the two, still exhausted from the fight, to handle the rest. Both shook their heads in disbelief of what just happened, their group leader unfettered by it. That always disturbed them; how calmly he dealt with things.

Sara and Klein looked at each other seeing the blood and bruises all over their bodies through ripped clothing and let out little laughs. It had been a long time since they were in a fight and this was more intense than any they'd ever been in. Picking up their gear, and whatever pizza wasn't ruined in the fight, they returned to headquarters. Not another soul could be found in the strip mall.

Traveling through the vortex, the manbeast visualized the safe house they had to reach once the vortex reopened at the exit. He made a mental picture of a room with the bare minimum of furniture, such as a bed, a table, a chair, and a small window. As they came out of the vortex, their bodies were spewed out. The hard landing was softened for Jared by the manbeast sheltering his body as they rolled to a stop. Still in shock, he laid on the floor staring at the ceiling. The manbeast picked him up gently then set him on the bed. His form was now mostly human, and he stood at six feet seven inches tall, his dark mane swept back from his face, with eyes the color of molten steel. Setting himself down in the chair across from the bed, he watched over Jared.

Charles

Inside the city, everything moved at a fast pace, meaning Charles had to act quickly. Contacts didn't stay put in one place for too long and his employer had ties with criminals of all sorts. One such place run by the organization's faction of the Yakuza was nearby.

Five young Japanese boys, all taller than their native country's average, lounged in front of the restaurant, sheathed Katanas in plain sight. Their conversation came to a halt when they saw Charles approach. Even seeing the organization's insignia on his sleeve, they were going to give him a hard time. He knew better than to show up there without permission and there was no information of any errands being run for their site today. The tallest of the five stood to his full height of six feet two inches and pushed his palm into Charles' chest.

"Uh-uh." The Yakuza boy waved his finger at him. "You not welcomed here."

"I just need some information." Charles had a main contact with many channels to be maneuvered before he could meet her. She was the boss' undersecretary and his sometimes lover. "Gomen'na sai." He bowed slightly.

The young man turned to his cohorts and nodded. Two grabbed him by the arms while the others went ahead to the back where their boss was. They shoved him into the office where he landed on both knees. He looked around with just his eyes, not making any sudden head movements. Slight rays of sunlight seeped through the tiny window near the ceiling of the back office making it dimly lit. The boys snickered amongst themselves hoping for a show when their boss arrived.

Yakuza bosses are very stylish, Charles thought as the owner of the restaurant came out from behind a beaded curtain.

His hair slicked back, secured in a tight ponytail, showed off his porcelain skin and distinct Asian features. The suit was an Armani, something Charles had a thing for and could identify on the spot. He felt a twinge of jealously.

"How much did that outfit set you back? I'm thinking of getting one next pay." Charles gave a crooked smile as he asked.

Two of the young boys hit him from each side in the ribs. It took the air out of him and he slumped over, his forehead touching the filthy carpet. Addressing the boss directly was stupid and he never did have a filter when it came to authority. He found it amusing, their sense of superiority.

"What did you come here for, trash?"

The owner was just as tall as his errand boys, towering over Charles and looking down on him with disgust.

"I just need to get a report to the Undersecretary but, you know…" Charles sat up and shrugged in defeat.

"No," the owner cracked his knuckles, "I don't."

Charles realized his plan of gaining an audience with the owner of the restaurant to locate his source was more complicated than anticipated. Too many questions were not looked upon nicely. He prepared to receive his information with a bloody nose and a couple of bruised ribs. It was an expected outcome, so he brushed it off and braced himself just as the owner plowed a fist into the side of his face. The owner asked him again.

"Why are you here?"

Charles gave a revised recount of the incident in the strip mall, leaving out transforming dogs and vortexes.

"My crew was ambushed in a strip mall by my territory. They got away and took one of my men. I sent the others to give a report."

"Is that so?"

The boss sniffed then resumed hitting him.

After giving Charles a brief reprieve from getting beaten, the owner nodded to his right-hand man standing near the curtain. He disappeared for about two minutes which made Charles a little nervous about his chances of escaping. When the thug came back, he whispered into the owner's ear.

"It seems you DO need to make a report, quickly." He nodded to the man who scribbled something on a piece of paper and threw it down by Charles' feet. "Get him out of here." He turned and went back through the curtain, his thug in tow. Charles left by air as two of the younger boys stood at the entrance and tossed him out onto the sidewalk.

Leaving the lively part of the city for the inner, he made his way to the rendezvous point. It was an old heap of a shed that sat unattached to the closed business next to it. He managed convincing one of the Yazuka boys to relay a message to the undersecretary about the location. At the entrance of the rundown shack sitting on the outskirts he peered through the rusted metal door to see if anyone was inside. Making sure the coast was clear, he entered and waited for her to arrive. He didn't have to wait long.

"What in god's name are you doing?"

She stormed in and came right up to him. The metal door wheezed in protest before banging shut. She wore a dark slate grey skirt suit with a two-button jacket and navy pumps. Her straight dark hair lay loose past her shoulder blades, the ends cut perfectly across as if a line had been drawn to separate her lower body from the upper. Her cupid shaped lips were pursed into two ruby slits. She was angry.

"Good to see you too."

He pushed his hands into the front pockets of his slacks.

"This is not funny!" She pointed a manicured ruby nail at him. "Did my guys report to the boss about what happened?"

"Yes, we heard, and you need to leave this alone and let us handle this."

"One of my guys was taken. And that thing that was our dog…"

"Look," she moved so close to him that they exchanged air, "I know this is all a bit crazy but if you just calm down."

"I am calm, I'm just angry."

She searched his face for some evidence of that and as usual found none. Charles did not show emotion. It unnerved her whenever she saw a dull uninterested look on his face, like the boss.

"Come with me and lay low for a while, okay."

Her voice was soothing.

They touched foreheads and after a few moments, he nodded. She could tell he needed some release after all the crazy shit going on so far. As she led the way to her car parked around back, she made eye contact with the two enforcers standing off to the side across the street. They nodded to her as she got into the driver's seat and knew they were going to report to the boss' liaison. No one could be allowed to run around knowing about what happened at a strip mall in the suburbs of their city.

Jared

"Where am I? What happened?" Jared sat up slowly from his position on the stiff bed. He was asking himself more than anything and was not prepared for an answer.

"Somewhere safe, for now."

The manbeast stood up and went to his side. His robes made a soft swishing sound as the bottom dragged across the wood floor.

Jared reared back further on the bed against the wall. He was too tired and too scared to fight, although not so far gone as to submit to whatever came next.

"I would never hurt you, Jared."

"How do you know my name?" Just as he asked it, he felt stupid. Of course, it would know his name. The thing had been his pet German Shepard for a long time. "What are you going to do with me? I mean, what the hell is going on?"

"If I said we were going to our home world soon, how would you feel about that?"

"Who are you? What are you?"

Jared was getting sleepy again, his words slurring with the slump of his body back to a lying position on the bed. It was all too much for his mind to bear.

"I am Modas and I am yours. We will explain when you feel better."

"We?"

Jared fell asleep. His body relenting to gravity and falling sideways on the bed.

Modas reached out his hand to move strands of hair from Jared's face then stopped himself. Not being able to convey how he was feeling at that moment tortured him. He sat back down in the chair and waited for the older woman to show up. From there everything would be set back right.

Small tingling sensations ran through his body as it settled into its original form, grateful to not be a pet dog anymore. It had been a demeaning existence because being a warrior meant more than anything, except as a father and mate. These thoughts went through his head as he too fell asleep dreaming of times past and what was to come.

Muted sunlight shone down on the fields of flowers while children ran through them laughing in merriment. Even with a weakened sun high in the hazy ochre colored sky, some slight warmth could be felt. Near the temple on the hill a bright orb appeared, shaking the ground. Workers and children stopped with bated breath at the entry.

Out stepped the old woman with the silver curly hair. She nodded to the guard standing at the console that controlled the transport gate without slowing her stride towards the temple. The children resumed playing in the fields and the workers returned to their duties. She smiled at them, knowing what everyone was thinking when the alternate gate opened.

In the temple, she quickly changed clothes then headed for the garden on the side of the structure. Many of her people toiled endlessly to keep the garden flush with energy to maintain the life held in suspense there. It was not a garden of plants. All the small buds of light were soul cores rescued after the disintegration of their home world. So much life had been lost. Once vessels were found for the cores, they would start a new cycle to rebuild their race.

The first step was to find the ones whose bodies were intact yet missing their original cores. They were scattered across different worlds and dimensions. Who the race really needed was their leader and the old woman had found him on Earth with three of his cabinet members. She had also found the monster who had destroyed their world. Bending down to stroke one of the glowing cores, her gaze fell across the garden. Soon, everything would be right. She got up and headed back to the gate for her travel to the safe house where Modas and Jared hid.

☼

Bright light jolted Modas out of his slumber and the chair he was sleeping in. It careened across the room into a wall as his body automatically crouched into a defense stance. Seeing it was the old woman, he relaxed. The vortex closed, and he sighed with relief.

"You frightened me."

"Who else would it have been? You are too on guard. No one knows about this place except us." She looked upon Jared. "How is he doing? I see he is still asleep."

"In shock still. Which there will be more of when we get his core back into him."

"You miss her greatly."

Modas kept silent. It needed no reply. He too, strolled through the garden from time to time checking on some of the cores that remained. He knew which ones were his family. Ganna motioned to Jared and Modas picked him up, cradling Jared in his arms.

"Let's hurry."

"What about our leader? Chardon could be in danger."

"I know, but my cover is compromised, as is yours, so we must be careful. I am sure you don't want to be a pet dog again."

"No." Modas shifted Jared's weight towards him. "I'm ready, let's go."

Janice slid out from underneath the covers and out of bed. With catlike movements she padded naked in silence to the living room. Finding her purse, she reached in, pulled out her mobile vidcom and dialed. A face appeared on the tiny screen revealing one of the boss' henchman. She leaned in closer to the screen and whispered angrily.

"What does he want me to do about Charles? He's asking a lot of questions in the wrong parts of town. I can't keep him locked down."

"Do nothing. Tell him you have a meeting with the boss and he is to stay put. We will come get him."

The smile on the henchman's face was crooked.

"Fine, I'll do that, but he's not stupid. If he senses something is wrong, he will run."

"Not your concern. We'll handle this. Do as you're told."

The screen went dark.

Placing the device back into her purse, she went to wake up Charles. He could at least have a decent breakfast before the enforcers came for him. At the bedroom doorway, she stopped for a moment to stare at his sleeping body under the sheets. She went over to the side of the bed and started kicking it lightly.

"Wake up, you. I'm hungry. What are you going to fix me?"

After the tenth kick, Charles stirred, turning his head to face her. She was beautiful with a well-proportioned athletic body and knew she did nothing for him emotionally. She was just a warm body to alleviate his tension when needed. He never cared about their relationship being against the rules. He sat up on his knees, letting the sheet fall back behind him and wiped his face with his hands.

"I thought you were going to cook for me."

"Alright, how about we do it together?"

"Sounds like fun"

"It has to be fast though. I have to meet the boss. He seems to want to talk to me."

"Good. Ask him about that creature I saw." He climbed out of bed to search for his pants. She raised an eyebrow at his nakedness debating on a second round and saw him tense up.

Not today.

Near the end of breakfast, she let out a deep sigh and turned to him.

"I need you to stay here until I get back."

"Why?" He set his spoon down in the half-eaten bowl of oatmeal.

"Because it's not safe, Charles. There are strange things running around and you talked to a few people who don't like being asked questions." Her finger extended at his nose. "So, stay put."

They finished up and went back to the bedroom to get dressed and make the bed. He had not answered her, and she kept glancing at him until he did.

"Fine."

He pushed off the edge of the bed, finishing the corners of the sheets by tucking them under. Relieved, she let him follow her to the front door.

"I'll call you when I am on my way back, okay."

She gave him a quick kiss and left.

Outside she could see in the corner of her vision four of the organization's enforcers waiting across the street for her to get in her vehicle and leave before moving in.

It was his own fault, she thought as she got in and pulled off.

Charles sat down on a stool at the black marbled island in the kitchen. He always wondered why her place was all black and stainless steel. It reminded him of an underground bunker. His thoughts went over the scene from the strip mall, finding it hard to believe less than forty-eight hours had past.

Midway through his mind drifting, it snapped back into reality as he noticed the silence. She lived on a pretty lively inner-city block and there was usually a lot of noise. No traffic or people could be heard and right about now he could probably hear a pin drop. Cursing under his breath, he made his way to the door and laid in wait for his attackers. If they were coming in hot, he had to be ready for a world of harm. It was not a long wait.

A New World

The weak sunlight still made Jared squint as he woke up in another bare room. He sat up and looked around surveying the area. So many questions were going through his head. He figured they would tell him what's what soon enough. Modas had stepped out of the vortex onto solid ground, setting him down right before the exit and he felt a little funny about it.

Was I really so out of it?

His conclusion was he must have been, remembering that he fainted not long after.

One thing was certain before he lost consciousness; this was not Earth. The air smelled different and the sky had a weird orange color, not blue. Even the grassy knolls were not quite green. What had made him pass out was the sighting of a strange little field creature that scurried across not far away.

Testing his footing on the floor, he went to the door and it opened to a hallway. He left the solitary room and headed down until reaching an archway outside. The grass was tall along the pathway and he brushed his hands against it as he walked. Near a clearing, he saw children laughing and playing in the fields. To the right of him was another path leading to a rocky area with a creek. He followed it, amazed at how bold he was going off on his own.

On a huge rock in the middle of the creek sat Modas in front of the waterfall. His mane of hair was swept away from his face and cascaded down his back to his waist. He wore a sleeveless thin bluish grey robe over a rough woven brown long sleeved one making him look like a monk. Modas meditated sitting akimbo and he was beautiful. Jared felt himself blush.

Modas must have felt his presence because he opened his eyes and turned towards him, not getting up.

"Are you feeling better?" Modas asked.

"I guess, if you consider I am on a different planet or something, sure." His own sarcasm felt wrong and he wondered why.

Ganna had apparently followed him out of the room and now came over to them. Her silver curls bounced freely around her shoulders. How could I not have seen or heard her? A feeling of uneasiness washed over him. Something about her, he didn't like.

"With you awake, we can begin. Shall we?"

Waving an arm in the direction of the temple was her way of requesting they both follow her. She led the way, walking briskly.

He began thinking in his head, No way that woman is old. Grandma has too much pep in her step.

A rundown temple came into view and they went in, heading towards the back, then turning to end up on the side of the structure. He saw the garden of glowing buds and inhaled with wonder. So enchanted, he went to touch them. Modas grabbed his wrist to stop him.

"Not yet. Please, wait."

Jared looked up at Modas with a confused face. Ganna sighed heavily, stepping next to Jared.

"My name is Ganna. I am one of the cabinet members here at the temple. Since the destruction of our world, what was left of the governing structure convened under the care of the few temple servants who had survived.

We conduct meetings here for convenience," she paused, chuckling, "and divine counsel. What you see before you in this garden are the souls of our fallen people, their cores. We were only able to save this many. Some of them need new vessels whereas for others, we need to find their vessels."

"Their vessels?"

"Their physical bodies," Modas interjected.

"Our consciousness, or soul, resides in our physical bodies. They can be removed if the body is too damaged to sustain it. Souls manifest as orbs of energy, as you see here, and can be reinstated in a new or repaired vessel. When our world was attacked, a vortex had been opened. Through that opening, many of our kind were thrown into other planes, other planets and other worlds which ripped their cores out of their bodies, leaving behind one or the other."

"So, you're searching all over the place. But, their, um, vessels could take a long time, right?"

"Time was not of importance until now. We have found at least some of the cabinet members and our leader, so there is hope."

"Why is time not important now?"

Jared felt like a broken record since Ganna was taking too long explaining for him.

"The one who destroyed our world knows we have survived. He is on that planet called Earth running some kind of crime ring, as they call it."

"Wait," Jared held up one hand having a thought. "Am I a hostage, like your ticket to get close to my boss?"

Modas looked pained while Ganna grimaced. Jared was confused.

He could not figure out what they wanted from him. Modas stepped into the garden, went about one hundred feet and picked up one of the glowing buds of energy. He came back and placed it in Jared's hands.

Almost instantly, Jared's entire body jolted, and memories flooded into him. Tears spilled down his face with every heart wrenching moment crashing against him making his grip tighten on the core until it made contact with his abdomen, forcing the core to slowly disappear into him.

Jared went down hard to the ground, his eyes rolled up in their sockets and he started to convulse. Modas held him down with all his strength because Jared had become incredibly strong. Ganna ran into the temple to find a healer. She grabbed one and ordered them to bring a sedative to administer. As the drug was injected into him and began to work, Jared ceased to move. Modas touched his face gently.

Jared's body slowly shifted back into its original form. His short dark hair turned light brown and grew to his shoulders, his features softened, and his skin went a shade darker. Breasts and hips swelled beneath the constricting human clothes, creating tears in the fabric. This form was female, and her name was Jaron.

Sara and Klein were escorted by three enforcers into the great hall of the mansion where they now stood. The entire room was stark white from floor to ceiling and smack in the middle against the far wall sat a giant white marbled throne. It seemed unreal, and a bit silly, to imagine their boss actually sitting on it dictating orders from above. Klein smirked, and Sara elbowed him in the ribs. A low grunt left his mouth. The side door had opened and out came the man himself.

The boss was tall and slender with straight pitch-black hair hanging to his waist. His sinister eyes were an odd color of dirty forest green. This man had killed, possibly murdered, many in his lifetime. Klein gulped. The boss walked slowly up to his throne and sat, throwing a leg over one side, his elbow resting on the other to hold his head as he cocked it sideways.

"So," he drawled, "I hear you had an encounter with some sort of manbeast. Tell me, what did it look like again?" An eerie hush fell on the room.

The two looked at each other and nodded.

"Well," Sara started, "at first it was our pet dog but then it changed into this bear like thing, but it changed again and had a lot of long hair and claws but a human face."

"Slow down," Klein whispered to her.

She was talking a mile a minute.

"You know, when I destroyed that putrid world of yours, I expected the two of you to go with it. Low and behold, here you are as my ignorant employees."

Klein's face wrinkled.

"What are you talking about?" He snapped.

He heard Sara gasp and immediately became surprised at his own boldness.

The boss threw back his head and let out a loud fit of laughter. No one else in the room joined in. Afterwards, he brought his head back and his eyes bore into theirs. It was clear he was not amused in any way.

"Do you know why your planet was destroyed? Because the two of you betrayed your own kind and opened the gate for me. You have no memories of it because your cores were ripped out. You're just soulless empty vessels doing my bidding. Shameful really."

They both stood stunned like two deer in headlights. None of what their boss was saying made any sense. To insinuate they betrayed someone causing the destruction of a planet was too much.

"You're lying! That's a lie!" Sara began to cry. Her body moved towards him and Klein stopped her. "We would never do something like that!"

She clamped her hands over her mouth in fear.

"No?" The boss slid his leg off the side of the throne, sitting upright, then leaned forward. Dark tresses of hair fell across his shoulders covering the white shirt he wore. "Such deceit the two of you had in you. And now your kind has scrounged up what is left of it to come and rescue its lost vessels. Should I let them take you? Have your souls returned to you? So, they can all know the truth about their demise?"

Klein shook with rage and confusion, grabbing Sara's hand. The boss sat back and waved his hand toward them.

"Get back to work, you haven't met your quota for the week."

"What about Charles and Jared?" Klein was scared yet some assertive streak had taken hold of him.

"Your fearless leader and his cabinet member? I am taking care of that. By the way, that creature, formerly your pet dog, is really one of the great beast warriors of your kind." He laughed again.

Jaron opened her eyes and focused on yet another bare room without furniture or windows. Turning her head to one side she saw Modas curled up in a chair next to the bed. His sleeping face caused a twinge in her chest. As much as she loved him, she was never able to show her affection. She did not disturb him. It pained her still.

Lost in her thoughts, she did not notice him awaken and their eyes locked. Having her core back was a curse and a joy. She remembered her time on Earth and the carnage left by the attack that destroyed her world. The heartache was much worse as she remembered the death of their children. She knew Modas could see it all on her face.

"Don't think of that. I can't bear to see you crumble anymore," he pleaded softly.

"How many?"

She barely whispered, fearing the answer.

"Jaron." Modas reached up to touch her face.

"How many?" She screamed, slapping his hand away.

"Three." Her face blanched. "Their cores are in the garden."

"Out of seven of our children, only three." Jaron sank down onto the bed and covered her face with both hands. "Only three." She felt Modas move from the chair and climbed on top of her, his body heat too warm. "Please, don't try to comfort me."

"I won't let you go."

He lowered himself onto her and rested his head in her bosom while she cried silently. His hands tightening into fists as he gripped the blanket beneath her.

The Big Boss

Undersecretary Janice paced around the anteroom chewing on her thumbnail. Seeing the boss had that effect on her from the day they met. Something about him was not quite right, like he didn't belong in this world. She had seen him do impossibly horrid things to people and swore to herself that none of it was real. Still, there were the nightmares.

"He is ready to see you now."

A grotesque looking enforcer had come to escort her. His features were off as if he was wearing human skin not fitted correctly.

"Thank you."

She turned around and with an air of authority hurried out to the throne room.

There he was, Halfar, lounging on his throne as usual with his left leg tossed over the side. He seemed bored and agitated at the same time, which would be impossible for a normal human being.

"I can smell him on you. Soap and water does not wash away a stench so powerful. How is Charles?"

He never even looked at her when he asked, unnerving her to the point of becoming scared. She wondered how he knew what Charles smelled. Her insides churned uneasily, making her nauseous.

"I would assume angry since your enforcers waited outside my place to pick him up." She heard her own voice quiver.

His gaze turned on her and she froze with fear. Those were the eyes of a monster.

"Are you questioning my methods?"

"Not at all, sir."

She gulped to clear the lump in her throat. He heard it.

"It would seem we underestimated Charles because he is not here. And neither are my enforcers. What do you think happened?"

"I..."

No words came to mind. It never occurred to her that Charles could defend himself against enforcers. "I'm not sure, sir. I left him there as instructed." She tried to conjure up an image of Charles taking on enforcers and failed. It was not feasible.

"Yes, it is." He replied, having somehow read her mind. She felt the color drain from her face. "I know Charles better than anyone here, yet I was not consulted about his little quest therefore I lost enforcers. Not even Charles knows how good he really is."

"I don't understand." She licked her lips. It was clear she had been left in the dark on something very important.

"Nor will you. You won't see him again. I am assigning you to another district effective immediately." She was about to protest, and he raised his hand. "Now."

As the undersecretary was escorted out, one of the boss' generals came into the throne room. He was not very tall at six feet two inches compared to the rest of the boss' entourage, but his body was all lean muscle. His wavy hair had a dark oily look and his eyes were an odd shade of amber. Tearing apart flesh was a specialty of his. It was rumored that his very presence made the other men's skin crawl. The boss sat correctly as a smile crossed his lips.

"What do you think, Rass? Shall we prepare for war?"

"Not likely." General Rass stood next to the throne and motioned for the room to be cleared. The long robe he wore laid open in the front but was secured around his waist with a thin sash, exposing his tight tunic and animal hide leggings. "That race is in shambles and it would be years before they can muster up the courage, let alone the numbers, to come at you with an army."

"I do not want to let Charles go."

"Hmm, well it may be beneficial if you do. He is easy to control because his core is missing, but that's not what you want. You want him whole again."

"Whole again, yes, but still under my thumb." The boss wagged his index finger at Rass.

"Who you need to worry about are those two imbeciles who betrayed their own kind. If they are capable of such treachery, then there is no doubt they will do the same to you."

The boss' right arm morphed into a giant reddish black claw with pincers that glistened as if dripping with blood and he snapped them once, the sound echoing within the room.

"Then I guess they will have to be sliced in half, hmm? Find Charles."

Rass gave a hideous smile. He went back through the door from which he came. Time to go hunting for insubordinates and bring them back for his own brand of sentencing, which he doled out with great pleasure.

"Charles." The boss closed his eyes remembering the last time they talked. "Chardon."

☼

A cloudy day, the sky signaling rain which would be good for the crops. He watched Chardon breathe in the fresh air then open his eyes to stare into Halfar's. As the ruler of his home world he traveled a lot. Going to see Chardon was for a personal agenda.

"You will not accept my proposal?" Halfar was tense.

"No. I will not submit to your terms just so you can enslave my race."

"It is not slavery, just safe keeping from harm of other more powerful forces."

"That is not what you are doing!" Chardon turned away from then glanced back.

"I can destroy you!" Halfar could feel himself shake with anger, regretting what he said.

"And, that is why you will never win."

"Listen to me! This will not end well. You know how she is!"

Chardon balled his hands and whirled on him.

"I know better than anyone." He hissed.

"No, you don't."

Halfar turned and walked out of the room.

Not long after that Halfar sent a planet destroyer through the portal gate Sara and Klein had given him access to. He opened his eyes, still burning with even more regret, and surveyed the empty throne room. It should not have happened. He truly wanted to protect them. His bruised ego made him react like a spoiled child, annihilating Chardon's entire world.

To the right of the throne, double doors opened and his other General, Kur, entered. His flowing locks of deep green hair bounced slightly around him as he strolled slowly towards Halfar, frowning at the expression on his lord's face.

"That is not the face of our cunning ruler. What could possibly make you look this way?"

"I haven't killed anyone in over three months."

Halfar made sure his face conveyed boredom. It was good to keep up appearances.

"Ahh, so I was mistaken, it being a lovelorn look. Surely, Rass is not slacking?"

His question drenched in sarcasm. Kur fancied himself having more flare than the crude and messy Rass.

"We must keep it down to a minimum or we lose allies."

"Allies! These disgusting, fragile humans? You must be joking! They are a means to an end for our race to take over and enslave them."

"True but they have a saying here I have grown fond of. You catch more bees with honey."

"What does that even mean?" Kur did not like being confused or taunted.

"How I understand it is we give them what they want, make them feel safe and when everything is in place, we take it all away. WE have to get them on board first."

"Sounds lovely. It does have a nice ring to it." Crude knotty wings a darker shade than his hair tore out of Kur's back and he knelt in a launching position. "I shall return with something good for you to play with." His body shot straight upwards towards the skylight, causing a funnel of wind to spiral after him. As he got close to the ceiling, it split in two opening up to let him through.

Halfar rose from his throne and went to the double doors on the left leading to his personal chamber. As ruler of his race, he knew what they expected of him. He was getting weary of being so ruthless and cunning.

He wanted peace. He wanted … love.

Extraction

Charles was cold, hurting and angry.

A lot of his energy was used to take those enforcers down and he had a few deep lacerations as a memento. Those wounds would heal after some time. Knowing that Janice had set him up was a whole other matter. One would think there was some level of trust when two people were intimate, that seemingly not the case. An ambush in broad daylight meant the organization didn't care about the laws of the land anymore.

As usual, the people in the neighborhood had hid themselves, leaving Charles to fend for himself. The only reason he got away moderately injured was the low level of the enforcers sent. He realized halfway into the fight how fast he was moving and how easy it felt. Still, those buggers fought him hard before going down. It was usually anything for the boss' glory. Charles was fighting for himself now.

Tearing more fabric off his shirt to tend yet another wound, he rose and peeked cautiously around the corner. The alleyway hid him well enough but not if enforcers were lurking. Those monsters could see through walls and Charles had not figured out how yet. Pulling the piece of cloth tight around his forearm with his teeth, he winced from the pain. At least the bleeding had stopped. It was clear to him that the boss wanted to speak with him, preferably alive but not necessarily undamaged.

"Shit, Charles, you need a plan," he said to himself as he crouched back down to think. His eyes went blank again, his face expressionless.

Ganna tapped the side of Modas' and Jaron's chamber door frame. She had left them alone for a few days after Jaron's full awakening. According to her patients who had gone through the process, getting back your soul was exhausting and the memories flooding in all at once took a toll. That was the consensus. She had never lost her core.

"How are you feeling, Jaron?" She found her up and about fixing the bed covers.

"A bit weary but more than anything, I'm angry." Jaron leaned over the bed to straighten up the pillows as the sleeves of her robe dragged across them. She was wearing the white and blue cabinet member robes. "To know that I was working for our enemy! He must have been full of smug joy ordering us around."

"Yes, well the dire matter at hand is getting Chardon and the rest out of there and back to this world so we can reinstate their cores."

"That should be easy since they are not in any danger."

"We are not certain of that. Since you were brought back and all of you did see Modas, it is safe to assume they reported the incident to their boss' henchmen. That means, Halfar knows we exist and may take drastic measures to keep them."

"Then we have no time. Do you have a plan in mind?"

"Besides going in blazing? Not really. I do have a way of pinpointing Chardon's whereabouts. Retrieving him comes first."

"When do we go?" Jaron stood upright ready to walk out with her.

"YOU do not. A small team will go through the gate and get him."

Ganna wagged her finger.

"Why not?" Jaron yelled.

"How are your powers?"

Jaron stopped advancing towards her and frowned. She lifted her right hand and a small orb of light blue energy formed.

"Damn it!" It shrunk, disappearing in the air.

"Give it time. For now, just rest and try to be nice to your mate. I never understood how he could love someone like you who always ignores him or treats him badly."

Jaron looked away and went to hide her face against a nearby wall. Ganna knew she didn't need to tell her that. It was a work in progress, especially now.

"Maybe he sees something in you that the rest of us do not." Ganna turned to leave. "At any rate, some bonding time is much needed. I won't need to report, we will all know when Chardon has arrived."

With that, she left realizing she had overstepped her boundaries. Jaron probably wanted to burn her to cinders. Ganna couldn't care less.

Out of the corner of her eye, Jaron saw Modas get up from the chair and head towards her. She stiffened for no reason and spun around to face him. He stopped, hesitant to continue, but followed through, grabbing her by the back of the neck to draw her close to him. He kissed her hard. She pushed him away, sending him across the room back near the chair he had just vacated.

"What are you doing? There's no time for that!"

The moment she pushed and yelled at him her heart felt great pain.

Why did I do that?

Watching Modas get up with no ill intent towards her

made it worse. He just stared at her, not saying a word.

"I need to assess the level of my power. Show me a vacant area on this world." Jaron hurried out the door, Modas not far behind.

A street vendor dropped his tongs in the filmy hotdog water, his mouth gaped open at the black hole appearing on the road in front of him. Warping inward like liquid it enlarged to a size big enough that four figures emerged from. Once they were securely on the ground, the vortex vanished. There was really nothing strange about them except their entry.

The vendor packed up and left the area without saying a word, pushing his cart down the street as fast as he could. In that part of town, crime was rampant, and no one bothered to notice since anything or anyone that might look bad was avoided. Nothing had been seen or heard if anyone asked.

The team nodded to each other acknowledging the situation was better than perfect. If a fight broke out between them and enforcers it would be a no holds barred brawl. It was best to avoid casualties and witnesses. A small ball of light formed in the leader's hand. They all looked at it to see how far Chardon was from their location. Finding him, they headed in that direction.

"I'm just having a really bad day, aren't I?"

Charles backed up from the group of enforcers forming a semi-circle around him.

"Come on, guys, it doesn't take this many of you for little old me." They were a good foot taller or more than him. Advanced group.

They all morphed at once and Charles saw what the enforcers really were. Their arms turned into various claw like appendages and their faces distorted into monstrous creatures. He looked around and noticed everyone who had been on the streets vanished. So much for someone calling for help. He was in deep trouble. As the enforcers bounded towards him, a bright light engulfed the streets.

The team saw the enforcers a block beforehand and took offensive positions. A surprise attack was the only way to win this fight and get Chardon back safely. A brutal fight ensued as the team went toe to toe with enforcers, tearing off limbs and tossing them haphazardly into the street. Their movements were a blur of colors and Charles had a repeat show of the strip mall fight. He noticed their technique was creating a clear path straight for him. Arriving at his side the team swooped in and grabbed him forcefully while collectively creating a vortex.

Charles had no time to think as his body was pulled through. He saw the carnage left behind and two enforcers still intact take pursuit. Whoever his saviors were, he was grateful and more confused than ever. All this from one little incident in a strip mall.

He hated strip malls.

Charles kept his mouth shut witnessing the gate open. It was almost funny. There was no reason for him to laugh in his situation. In reality, it wasn't funny in the least. All the same he wanted to burst out loud. Monsters, vortexes, strange powers and what not. He felt his body slow down as they approached the exit and he could see fields of strange tall plant life swaying in the wind behind a male figure standing at what looked like a console. As his feet hit solid ground, the vortex closed and the male figure bowed down on one knee to him.

"Now I know something is not right."

He turned to his saviors and saw they too had gone on

bended knees. "Please, get up. This is embarrassing."

"It is only fitting that we should bow to our leader." Ganna stepped out from the shadows. "Welcome home, Chardon."

She bowed down low.

"Leader my ass! What the hell is going?"

He felt a twinge of anger. Being kept out of the loop irritated him.

"Forgive me, I will explain immediately."

"You bet your ass, you will! And my name is not Chardon!" Though it seemed to fit as he heard himself say it.

"But, it is. Tell me, do you have any memories from before you worked for your organization?"

"What? Of course I…!"

Charles stopped, his eyes wide. He didn't, and it never occurred to him.

"Come, walk with me."

Ganna held out her arm and Charles took it, letting her lead the way.

"This is some crazy shit."

Looking around at the environment, he shook his head. The tall grass was a strange orange color with tiny off-white flowers at the base. Looking up, he saw the murky sky with its weak sun. Something that reminded him of a guinea pig, except with spiraled horns and a long alligator like tail, scooted across their path. This was definitely not Earth.

People all around him stopped what they were doing and bowed low to him. He was getting annoyed. As they made their way to what looked like a temple, he noticed the scenery did not match. There were newly constructed buildings right alongside clearly dilapidated ones. Once they entered the temple, Ganna led him to the garden.

She began to tell the story of Lassa's destruction, giving the short version as he made it clear he had no patience for details. He remained silent throughout the explanation of how the original planet had been destroyed. His brow furrowed with each word. Afterwards, she moved into the garden of cores.

He stood on the edge of the core garden letting the vast knowledge of what those glowing buds of energy were. To see the embodiment of souls clustered in one place left him shocked and saddened. His feet moved on their own, steering his body into the garden towards the center where he stopped in front of a core pulsing brighter than all the others with a rainbow of energy.

With trembling hands, he picked it up and held it to his body, slowly letting it meld into him. His head snapped back, causing him to fall to his knees in the dirt. All his memories came to him in a rush, mingling with his experiences on Earth, making him whole again. An urge to fall unconscious swept over him and he fought through it, eventually able to stand. His vision changed, with clearer focus.

Energy swirled around him like wisps of smoke, lighting up the fields. Workers and children stopped to witness the event while Ganna steadily backed away from the buzzing air. A giant orb of light formed outward from his body to engulf a thousand feet radius, tiny sparks shimmering around the edges. He could see everyone staring, mesmerized by the display. When all the energy and lights subsided, Chardon took a deep breath and slowly exhaled.

"Most usually lose consciousness when they are re-established with their core." Ganna kept her distance as she spoke.

"I am not most." Chardon turned to face her. "I feel

better already, but mostly I am angry."

"Jaron said the same thing. She wanted to be the one to come and extract you from that world."

"Is that so? Why didn't she?"

"I seem to have not regained my full power." Jaron came up to the garden's edge.

"It will come back soon enough. Are you treating Modas well?" He watched the struggle play on Jaron's face. "I guess there is a learning curve when it comes to love."

"We need to get Sara and Klein, too. I'm sure Halfar is going to have them on a short leash now that he knows we survived."

Chardon nodded in agreement, contemplating how to get his other cabinet members out of the demon's stronghold. Halfar was not to be underestimated. There was no way he would turn them over without a fight and Chardon was not yet ready for another. Despite his wounds having healed instantly when his core was returned he could still feel them. Enforcers were nasty creatures who obeyed Rass and Kur more so than Halfar. He speculated it was because Halfar didn't like getting his hands dirty these days.

"For now, they are safe. Halfar would not jeopardize a potential meeting with me by harming one of my kind. No, he sees this as a second chance."

Sara and Klein

Sara and Klein walked accompanied yet again by guards to the throne room. That room had such a horrible feeling to it despite the pure white interior, throne included. White symbolized purity in most cultures and Klein knew the boss had somehow bastardized it. As they entered the room, Rass greeted them with a slow bow and a sheepish grin. To the left of the room, were two men, on their knees wearing disheveled clothes, looking scared shitless.

"Good morning, my little traitors. I thought you would appreciate some entertainment before breakfast." The boss lounged on his throne as usual. "Rass, what have we got today?"

"Two dealers who were not only insubordinate but, tried to make a profit off the merchandise in the tune of a quarter million."

"Is that so? Hmm."

The boss tapped his index finger to his temple for a moment.

Klein had a bad feeling about what was about to happen. He always wondered how the room stayed so white. Someone had to clean it daily. Why? The answer became clear.

"Sara, close your eyes," he whispered urgently.

The boss had heard him.

"No! You will both witness my judgment." Leaning further back into his throne, he declared, "Skin them," with no emotion or fanfare.

Rass' hands grew into talons two feet long and just as the first man started to scream, one of the talons pierced his chest running down it like a scalpel. The other man screamed and cried, begging for mercy as blood from his partner splattered on him in waves. The skinning was done slowly and when the screaming had gone on too long for everyone's taste, the boss' arm became a huge claw reaching across the room to snap the dying man's head clean off. His partner stopped screaming out of sheer terror, defecating himself. Rass continued the skinning of the now decapitated dealer with utter delight.

Sara vomited on her own feet, slumping to the floor as she slipped in it. Klein could not move to help her back up. His mind had unhinged looking at the boss, who watched with an expression of disinterest on his face. Klein's eyes burned with such hatred, he felt ill.

Halfar stepped down from the throne, stood in front of the traumatized dealer and punched through his rib cage with the claw. He snapped the claw shut as it tilted up, cutting the dealer in half from sternum to head. Only the lower body remained. Halfar returned his hands to human form and sat back down on his throne dripping blood down the armrest.

"You see, I do have some sense of mercy. Don't you think?" A smile crept on his face.

"Monster," was all Klein could utter.

"Humph. Go, you will be late for morning roll call, and breakfast."

Two enforcers picked Sara up from the floor, her body limp in their arms. The other two yanked Klein away to the exit. The left side of the throne room lay covered in red. He felt sorry for whoever had to clean that macabre scene.

"Bring in the horde." Rass instructed the guards.

There was no need for Klein's pity. The double doors to the right opened to reveal a cluster of hideous monsters salivating from the smell of blood. Upon seeing the carnage, they rushed for it, slopping up blood and pieces of flesh. The sounds were horrifying to the human ears and Halfar again showed mercy by letting the human guards leave the room. A handful of enforcers stayed to join the festivities. Klein conjured up every grain of his sanity, so he could remember this day.

Halfar stayed until the end, hating every moment of it. It was a barbaric ritual at best and it did nothing to entertain him anymore. This was a lashing out on his part for losing Chardon. He should have known a team would be dispatched to get him and now Halfar was down eight enforcers in one fell swoop. Deep in thought, he did not notice Kur enter the throne room. When he did, Kur was staring at him, questioning. If there was one who didn't need to know what Halfar was thinking it was Kur. He averted his eyes in a weary sort of way to signal that he was bored and nothing more.

Kur was not convinced. He felt something was amiss with his ruler since the destruction of that backwards world he favored. Keeping the only known survivors was not Kur's choice, preferring the entire race be extinct. Not knowing why Halfar wanted to embrace them, he had a hunch the key was Chardon. Kur left the room, also bored of the bloody scene whose screams had lured him to investigate. There was no finesse at all in Rass' punishment.

"We have to get out of here," Sara hissed her words like a snake. She paced the length of her tiny room the organization supplied to low level runners and dealers. "He's going to kill us!"

Her face, still pale from vomiting, was now clean and she had changed her shirt.

"I don't think so." Klein stood legs wide apart, his right hand cradling the side of his face.

"How can you think that? Did you see?"

"Of course I did!" Her tone irritated him.

"Do you remember what he said about us?" Sara stopped pacing and stared at him in confusion. He sighed. She was not too bright to begin with so probably wasn't listening to the boss. "If what he says is true then that means Charles and Jared are going to try and rescue us. We can be free of him."

"That was just some bullshit he spouted to scare us."

"Umm, did you not see Jared's pet dog turn into a huge creature and some old lady make a vortex they all disappeared in?" He raised one eyebrow.

"But, we caused our world to be destroyed? He said that, didn't he?"

So, she was listening to some degree. Klein shook his head to clear out the numbness in his head created by her absentmindedness.

"They don't know we are the reason. We're traitors, right?"

"So," Sara walked closer to him, "we can get to our world, get our cores back and then high tail it out of there before anyone finds out what we really did."

"You are assuming we would know how to create one of those black holes. And go where exactly?"

"Oh." She looked like a deer in headlights, her mouth slightly open in the shape of her word.

Klein now saw how their supposed plan had failed and an entire race nearly wiped from the universe. This was his partner in crime? Holy Toledo. He decided to make amends, if possible. There had to be a reason why the two of them had sided with the boss, betraying their own kind. To figure it out, they needed their original cores. It would be easy to play dumb for now because they really just had the boss' word regarding their treachery, and he took that with a grain of salt.

"Don't say a word." His mind made up.

"About what?"

Sara's head cocked to one side.

Klein rolled his eyes.

"To Charles or Jared, do not say anything about what we may or may not have done in our original lives."

"Oh." Again, that deer in headlights look or had her expression not changed from before?

"We have chow, let's go."

"I am NOT eating!"

"We still have to go, genius."

He pulled her along out the door.

Chardon was not happy to see the core count for the garden. So many of his people died on a tyrant's whim. Entire families were wiped out, the planet scorched black. He could see it in his memories as the last thing known. A creak from behind alerted him to another presence in the room and he turned to find Modas silently entering. For such a massive beast, he was quite stealthy, and dangerous.

"Is Jaron being unreasonable again?"

"She's just frustrated that she has to work so hard to regain her power."

"Did she really think it would be that easy?"

"And there is the loss of our children."

Chardon looked away. He had heard about what remained of their litter. How heart breaking it must have been to learn that. His wife, Sestis, was also among the dead, her core destroyed with the planet. Luckily, he had no children to mourn.

"I believe this is a perfect time to start over until most of the vessels are found. We can create new ones for the cores left without one. If you play your cards right, she may be willing."

"It's not about if she is willing or not. That will happen regardless. It's that she's full of vengeance, her actions seem desperate."

"You can't blame her for that." Chardon faced him. "I also want justice for all this and knowing I was a tool, a play thing, for Halfar on Earth makes me angry." Modas nodded in agreement. "I have never known you to speak this much, Modas."

"Only when it's necessary." The manbeast left the room just as silently as he came in.

Chardon turned his attention to the sky. The weak sun spoke volumes to the condition of their new home. Chardon knew his race needed to adapt for a century or two before they found a new world to inhabit. A not so great planet trumped a dead one. He still didn't understand how the planet destroyer got through the gate. It bothered him as he checked his memories seeing how the blast came rushing across the land, disintegrating everything in its path, spreading like fire.

How did the gate get opened from the outside? Did Halfar figure out how from his last visit to their world?

For now, Chardon had one mission: to get Sara and Klein off Earth and back to this world. They had to be a little frightened by now since he and Jaron had not reappeared. This time he would go with a team of six knowing Halfar would not be naïve to send just a handful of enforcers again.

"Any luck?" Ganna had crept up behind Jaron who was practicing making orbs of energy in her hands.

"As a matter of fact, yes."

Showing proof, she expanded a ball of light and sent it outwards, letting it go wide into the trees. Off in the distance, the ball of destruction splintered one.

"Did you really have to destroy that tree? It meant you no ill will."

Jaron laughed.

"I will have another one planted and matured."

"It may take more time on this planet with its weak sun."

"I had forgotten." Jaron felt a twinge of regret over the former tree. This was not their home world. She glanced up at the sky noticing how it did not harm her eyes. "We can't stay here."

"It will do for now. Come, we're ready for a meeting on how to get Sara and Klein back."

"Excellent! I want to try my hand at eliminating some enforcers." She went around Ganna and together they headed for Chardon's chamber.

The Return of the Traitors

Halfar sensed the vortex opening almost instantly and summoned Rass to handle the situation. His henchmen were in the process of locating Sara and Klein who had skipped out on an errand and were currently on the run. Chardon's team getting to them first didn't bother him in the least. Those two had to face a very angry council of their people. Halfar smiled a little at that.

Would Chardon forgive them? Of course, he would because he is merciful, Halfar thought to himself.

It was a trait he himself had learned about some time ago. Ten enforcers were dispatched with Rass. He had a feeling only half would come back intact.

Like a scene from a sci-fi horror movie, the now vacant inner-city streets were showered in colored lights blazing across the sky along with bloody pieces of unknown origin. Some of it rained down on a few pedestrians still in the process of taking cover. No screaming was heard, just the sickly wet sounds of a massacre. Large cavities were blown out from nearby buildings, sidewalks sunk in towards the middle of the street and blood splattered everywhere.

Chardon came prepared for a fight. Not like this. Jaron was keeping enforcers at bay on the opposite side of him and the other four team members were fighting for their lives. They had located Sara and Klein easy enough and were ready to move out when enforcers showed up. Sara was crouched on the ground with her hands covering her ears while Klein's eyes darted about, possibly looking for a pathway into the middle where he and Jaron were.

For the second time, Chardon realized he was near a rundown strip mall. How ironic, he grimaced. The fighting was going in their favor until he saw Rass coming at him from the mall's direction. Summoning his energy to form a barrier, he barely made it in time as Rass slammed into it, trying to break through. Chardon pushed the field forward and Rass flew backwards away from him, landing on his praying mantis like legs with hatred in his eyes.

"Come to take your traitors back?" Rass yelled, blowing strands of black oily hair from his eyes.

Chardon, Jaron and the rest of the team were able to quickly glance at each other as they continued fighting. He saw Klein wincing with his hands clasped together in prayer.

"Oh, yessss," Rass hissed, "didn't you know it was them?"

He launched himself back into the melee targeting Jaron this time, landing a blow. She was knocked into the side of a building, some of the bricks crumbling from the impact.

"Is that what Halfar told you?" Chardon asked as he went to shield Jaron, only to be attacked from behind. He felt the talons of an enforcer slice through his back.

"Of course, they have no memory of it since their cores are gone." Rass laughed as Chardon saw two other team members get raked across their bodies by four enforcers, two on each side.

"Then it's his word against theirs?"

"Halfar doesn't lie." Rass spat.

Which was true, and Chardon knew that. He may never speak what's on his mind but if you asked him, he would tell you.

"No matter, I am going to slice all of you to pieces and serve you to him on a platter!" He again launched himself towards them.

A vortex opened and out of its gaping mouth sprung Modas meeting Rass midair to strike him down into the pavement, which caved in as they landed. Standing up, Modas spun around, grabbed Jaron and threw her into the vortex. In two steps, he had Sara and Klein, doing the same. Nearing Chardon, he nodded to the team and they all leapt into the vortex. They were able to hear Rass screaming in angry dissatisfaction before the closed vortex silenced it.

Halfar conjured up energy in the palm of his hand to create a viewing orb and watched the battle as it ensued. Out of ten enforcers, six were intact. Although glad, he didn't like that Chardon himself had come. If he had known, Halfar would have gone to retrieve him instead. Seeing Rass go into a fit of rage over defeat almost made him laugh.

"How childish and uncouth," Kur said as he entered without Halfar knowing yet again. He stood watching the scene as well. "He really has no flair for getting the most out of a battle."

"He has his own way of doing things. We can't all be as pristine as you, Kur."

"You would think he had learned something from me by now." Halfar dissolved the energy and the scene faded. Back in a lounging position on his throne, he watched, out of the corner of his eye, Kur trying to decipher what bothered him about his illustrious ruler. Halfar would tell him if asked. That would take the fun out of it.

"What will you do now that the remaining survivors have reunited to wage war against us?" Kur asked.

"Nothing. Do you really think a small group of a nearly extinct race can win against an army such as ours?"

"Stranger things have been known to happen."

"Not that." Halfar slid off his throne and headed for the double doors leading to his chamber. "Please make sure to congratulate Rass on his magnificent defeat."

Kur grunted as he turned and left through the main door at the center. He would do just that by challenging him to a duel out of spite. It was going to be a productive evening for his generals.

Sara and Klein hit the ground hard as they landed from their toss through the vortex. It was apparent that Modas had such violent force when it came to battle. Klein hit his head on the stone console in front of him as he tried to get up. Sara was in tears from sustaining scrapes and cuts from her fall. Behind them, Ganna was tending to Jaron just as Modas, Chardon and the team stepped out of the vortex onto solid ground.

A group of people in brown robes came rushing out to meet them, taking great care of Jaron and Chardon. Two of them came upon Sara. In her madness, she started screaming repeatedly, "Don't touch me!" Klein frowned and turning, punched her so hard, she fell back to the ground unconscious. The two in brown robes stared at him in awe, eyes wide, then picked her up and carried her away.

"That was a bit uncalled for, Klein." Chardon seemed angry, not necessarily at him.

"Yeah, well, would you have done it better?" Klein shot back as he rocked onto his feet.

"You do know I want the truth from both of you?"

"I don't see how, our cores were destroyed, right?"

For the first time, he realized how different Chardon looked from before, and the extent of his battle wounds.

"Right?"

Chardon turned to Ganna.

"Find their cores and return them to me."

"Of course." She bowed low and headed for the garden.

Klein sat back on his haunches in a daze, not sure if it was a blessing or a curse. Now he had a chance to make amends or be persecuted. He wondered what his original self was like and if Sara was just as irritating as she was now. Looking up at the sky into the weak sun he made his resolution.

Sara woke up flinging herself out of the bed she lay on, gasping for air. The left side of her head was in pain and she held fast to it rocking back and forth hoping to ease the burning sensation. In a flash, she remembered Klein had socked her there and with a rage not felt before she went into a fit, arms flailing about her, as she screamed at the top of her lungs. Abruptly, she stopped, realizing someone else was in the room with her.

Modas sat across the room watching her with no emotion on his face. He stared into her eyes and she saw what real fury looked like. Not the passionate burning kind, the cold unfeeling kind. He could murder me right now, she thought. He didn't say a word. It was like he had heard her thoughts and his eyes concurred. Seeing him up close, she noticed how large and formidable he was.

Where is Klein?

Now would be a good time for him to come to her rescue. She scanned the room, hopeful.

"Klein is with Chardon." Modas continued to stare at her, his eyes never wavering.

She almost said, oh.

Knowing how much it irritated Klein it would probably do the same for Modas. Her lips were parched so she licked them with her nearly dry tongue. It hurt.

"Will he be back soon?"

"That depends on Chardon."

"You know, the boss may have been lying about us being traitors, you know? I mean, we don't have any memories or anything because of our cores or whatever," she rambled out.

"Fascinating." Modas rose from the chair in disgust.

"What?"

Sara felt like she had been slapped in the face and insulted at the same time.

"Even without your core, you are still just as arrogant and selfish, as a woman."

Sara sat up straight and turned her nose up at him trying to appear unafraid. She was about to make a snide remark when what he said at the end rung in her ear.

"Huh?" She hiccupped.

Three medical sages tended to Chardon, bandaging his rib cage and treating the wounds on his back. From what Klein had heard, they would be healed by tomorrow and the healers were being cautious. The enforcers who injured him before were low level and did not cause much damage. In the last battle, they were henchmen of Rass and deadlier. Chardon winced as one of the medics pulled the bandage tight. Klein listened to him vow payback in the worst way for Rass and his band of enforcers. He was glad Halfar himself did not show up, or Kur for that matter.

Klein sat on his knees silent as the murky dawn. Chardon seemed angry about the treachery except more upset about the fact that Klein had taken Halfar's word without argument.

"So, despite not having any memories of who you

really are, let alone traitors to your race, you believed every word Halfar told you?"

Feeling ashamed, Klein nodded with his eyes squeezed shut. How stupid. It never crossed his mind that the boss might be lying. Something inside him knew it was true.

"Please, no matter what happens, I want to make amends. I really do."

"And how are you going to do that?" Chardon's eyes went wide. "Our world is dead!"

Klein flinched back and hung his head lower. He knew there was probably no redemption for him. Doing nothing was not an option. He sucked in his chest, raised his head and said, "Give me back my core and I will prove myself to you. I will be able to tell you everything."

Chardon waved off the medics, standing over Klein as he rose. "I have an idea of what happened and yes you will tell me why. First we will go get your lover and head to the garden."

"My lover?" Klein was confused for a moment, then his face paled. "You don't mean Sara?" He heard Chardon sigh. "What's in the garden?"

"Klein, get up."

Everyone headed out with Klein picking up the rear.

At the garden, Sara was like a kid at a petting zoo. A lot of "Ooh's" and "Ah's" escaped her lips as she stood on the edge staring at the glowing buds. Klein was not so enamored because he understood what those things were. It pained him to see so many yet so little left of their race and he didn't even have his core back yet. He turned to Sara.

"Stop that!" He was seething with anger. "Do you even know what you're looking at?"

"Why are you yelling at me? And why are you so angry?" She yelled back.

"Tell her!" He directed Ganna.

"Cores." Was all she said, and that snapped Sara out of her stupor.

"All those?" She whispered, and tears formed at the corners of her eyes.

A worker came up to Klein with a core in his hands giving it to him. Klein cradled it in his arms like a newborn and let it sink into him, disappearing. The jolt to his body was so severe even Sara jumped back in fear. He fell to the ground face down convulsing. Tears poured out of him as both memories intertwined. He could do nothing except lie there and take the brunt of it all. Medics rushed to him and used light energy to ease his suffering before taking him away.

Sara started shaking her head back and forth.

"No, no, no. No!"

Another worker was coming towards her and she knew it had to be her core. This is not what she wanted. She wanted to go back to Earth where it was relatively safe aside from the part where Halfar's organization was taking over the whole damn United States. She tried to back up as Ganna got behind and held her still while the worker touched her abdomen with the core.

As it entered her, she understood what Modas meant. Memories of a young man laughing with Klein, talking with Klein, kissing Klein flooded in and her body began to shift into that man. It did not take long, the pain excruciating as bone and muscle reconfigured.

The body thrashed about in convulsions, gurgled shrieks emitting from the mouth. With the transformation complete, he sprung forward into a sitting position and let out a scream so loud the nearby trees vibrated. Then he passed out. Two more medics came for him.

Chardon and Ganna glanced sideways at each other and she giggled. "How dramatic," Ganna quipped. "Talas always made things more entertaining than necessary."

"Humph. I think it will be interesting to know how Talas felt about being a female Earthling."

"I find it interesting that they were not lovers on Earth as they were here."

"That is curious. Klein seemed to barely tolerate her instead of having any affection."

"Well, tomorrow we will get answers. Modas and Jaron should be kept at bay."

"No, they need to be there to hear what these two have to say. I will stop them if they try to kill them."

"Good to know."

TWO:

Homeward

The throne was awash with black blood as Halfar entered. He cocked his head to one side to ask why as he made eye contact with Kur standing covered in his own green blood mingled with the thick purple of another, turning it black. Hence, the mess. Near the double doors on the left where Halfar had just come through lay Rass in a crouched position breathing heavily covered in the same mixture.

"We were having a slight disagreement on strategy, my lord." Kur bowed in jest.

"I will not be made a mockery of!" Rass was ready to launch.

With one swish of his arm, Halfar knocked Rass into the wall near the main entrance and headed towards Kur. He was not going to tolerate such nonsense without approval.

"I was just congratulating him on his defeat as you instructed."

Kur's voice was cut short by Halfar's claw clamping around his neck, lifting him off the floor. He knew the look in his eyes let Kur know that he had overstepped his boundaries.

"My apologies," Kur gasped and Halfar let him go.

"Clean this mess before I get back."

"Where are you going?"

"Since I am unable to use my throne room, I will have to settle for a stroll into the city."

Kur and Rass' eyes went wide with fear. That was never a good idea in any circumstance.

"You can't be serious!" They both exclaimed in unison.

Halfar turned to them.

"I need to blow off some steam, don't you think?"

With that, he left.

Rass ordered some of his guards to clean the mess, as did Kur, and they both hurried after him in an attempt to stop him, leaving a bloody trail down the hall. The last time Halfar went into the city he ended up destroying a five-block radius because a taco vendor mouthed off to him for not buying before eating. Trying to explain that to the authorities was not something to be desired. Yes, they were not of this planet and could annihilate it on a whim. That was not on the agenda for a few years yet.

"Please, my lord, we are deeply sorry. Come and relax for a moment." Rass talked fast.

"Where would that be?"

"The garden is in full bloom. Don't you want to see how our native flowers are doing in this wretched planet's soil?" Kur also talked as fast as he could.

Halfar stopped walking.

"They were planted?"

They halted a few feet away from him.

"Of course, my lord."

"When?"

"Nearly three months ago," Kur squinted as he thought, guessing.

"Then let us go see how they are faring before I go out."

"This way, please."

Rass bowed deep and waited for Halfar to pass before following, shooting Kur a dirty look as they both closed in behind him. Halfar knew they were relieved that some mass destruction had been averted so far.

Kelin lay resting on a bed weary and deep in thought. It was funny that Halfar had given him the human name Klein, seeing the similarities. If it were not for the ruckus going on in the room nearby, he would have rested for a few more hours. He could imagine one person having such a fit and it was none other than Talas.

Sitting up with the weight of his upper body supported by his elbows he let his head flop backwards. Every muscle in his body felt strained and he just wanted to stay in bed. That was now impossible with Talas thrashing about next door, so Kelin flung the covers off and marched over.

"For the love of Lassa, shut up!"

There were at least seven people in the room, him included and he felt like an imbecile. Everyone stood in place staring at him. Talas, still shaking with fury, advanced on him.

"Talas," he warned him.

Too late. Kelin fended him off by putting him in a choke hold before he could get any closer. They wrestled to the floor and as Kelin held him steady he said, "It's alright. There's no need to fight." He felt Talas relax then start sobbing quietly.

"I would ask if this was a good time for your confessions, but it seems that is not the case."

Chardon had entered the room followed by Jaron, Ganna, Modas and three other cabinet members. Jaron could hardly contain her rage. It poured out of her entire body.

"There is no good time for it so now is better than never." Talas lifted himself from Kelin, wiping away tears, to confront them head on. "I know what we did was unforgiveable, and it cannot be fixed. All I can do is pledge my loyalty to my kind, never to waver under promises and false hopes. So, I beg you."

Talas went down on his knees and bowed low, his forehead nearly touching he floor, "please, forgive me."

Kelin, still down on the floor, sat in awe of Talas. Especially when Jaron stepped forward to look down on him and slammed her fist into Talas' face as he looked up at her. Everyone else in the room flinched.

"Do you feel better now?" Chardon asked Jaron.

"No! Not in the least." Jaron ran out of the room, Modas in tow.

"Shall we begin?"

Chardon motioned for everyone to take a seat within the chamber, instructing Talas with a finger to wipe the blood from his mouth. He looked toward Kelin and nodded.

The Agenda

Lassa Fifty years ago

Once more Halfar came with his entourage in tow to negotiate submission to his Armada. The cabinet members were angry, keeping their tongues, all but one: Talas. Due to his outbursts, Chardon had ordered him out of the council chamber and the meeting adjourned for a little while. Sestis, Chardon's mate, found Talas pacing in a full rage near the grain field.

"You know this will end badly." She said sweetly.

Talas halted his pacing and regarded her with contempt.

How dare that monster speak to me!

He did not move an inch as she came closer. As revered as she may be, Talas knew she was capable of awful things. He just didn't have any proof.

"Our leader is going to get the entire race killed and all of you are going to let him."

"Better dead than slaves for that monster," Talas spat.

Sestis laughed. "It doesn't have to be that way. I have a proposal." "What is it, then?" Being in her presence alone agitated him.

"I believe we can coexist. I propose there be a delegate to oversee our kind to ensure it continues."

"We have a leader."

"One who does not see reason and humiliates one of his own cabinet members in front of the enemy?"

She shook her head looking mournful. Talas' eyes went downcast and he clenched his fists at his sides. "That was uncalled for to say the least." She moved closer to Talas. "I believe you can make him aware of his short comings."

"How?"

Talas seemed uneasy. This was Chardon's mate.

Did she really have their race's best interest at heart?

"When Halfar invades this world, I shall negotiate to appoint you and one other to rule over our race. Chardon will be at Halfar's palace and no longer leader. That would put him in his place, don't you think?"

"You would do this?"

"Of course. But, only if the invasion is a success." Sestis walked off into the distance towards her entourage of handmaids, who were just released from the council chamber to fetch her and smiled.

Talas stood in the same spot for a long time, delusions of grandeur dancing in his head. There was only one person who was meant to rule with him and that was Kelin. He needed to convince him that Sestis was right about making the invasion go smoothly to avoid loss of lives. It took only a few months to do so.

"You will not accept my proposal?" Halfar was livid.

"No. I will not submit to your terms just so you can enslave my race."

"It is not slavery, just safe keeping from harm of other more powerful forces."

"That is not what you are doing!" Chardon turned away from him.

He was not amused.

"I can destroy you!" Halfar shook with anger.

"And, that is why you will never win!"

"You will regret this."

Halfar hurried off with his entourage to the gate escorted by Modas' personal army. As they waited for the guardian to open a vortex, he saw Talas and Kelin nearby motioning him away from the not so watchful eye of the guardians towards them.

"I take it didn't go too well." Kelin was not surprised.

"It can still be accomplished." Halfar had a monstrous idea in his head and didn't dare reveal it. "If you can open the gate in three days, I can send my Armada through with directions to help you with transition."

"Transition for what?" Talas anxious.

"For the cohabitation, of course," He replied sweetly, "and the naming of their new rulers." Making sure to stare at them until they got the point.

"Three days?"

"Three days." Halfar saw the gate had been opened. His entourage, and he, marched through.

Once he arrived back on his own world, Halfar turned to his two generals, Rass and Kur, eyes burning with rage. They were surprised since he seemed to like that pathetic world.

"Prepare a world ender. I want it sent through the moment that gate to their world opens."

Kur raised an eyebrow. "Is there a radius you wish to declare?"

"NO! Scorch it all, the entire world."

"As you wish, my lord." He headed for the arsenal to inform their scientists to prepare the bomb.

"Are you sure?" Rass stopped not four feet from him to whispered it.

"Get it done!" Halfar nearly ran to his chamber doors, flinging them open with such force, a gust of wind blew Rass back.

"Are you sure this is what we want?"

Kelin stood over the guardian he had knocked unconscious as Talas worked the console.

"This is the best way to ensure our survival and plus, we will be able to rule over our race however we see fit. Chardon won't have a say anymore."

"Let's just hurry and get this done."

A vortex began to form at the center of the gate and they braced themselves for the armada that was sure to come in full force.

With a jolt of fear and regret, Halfar sat up from his bed and gasped.

"No, no, no!" He hurried out into the corridor and screamed, "Wait!"

"What is it, my lord?" Rass came briskly to him. "Chardon! You need to get Chardon!"

"I am sorry, my lord, but the planet destroyer is already traveling through the vortex."

Halfar grabbed Rass by the neck, lifting him off the ground.

"You will do this."

He let Rass go and returned to his bed chamber. Rass stood for a moment trying to figure out why his ruler would request such a thing then gave up and went to see what he could do. There was a way, and he was sure Halfar would still be grateful, regardless of the outcome.

Children played in the fields, warriors were in the middle of their daily training, the high council was in a meeting and the sun shone down on them all unaware that Kelin and Talas were opening the gates of Hell. Both stood proud ready to greet their new allies. Chardon had skipped the council meeting to tend a fruit patch when he felt the vortex.

The gate opened.

Heat shot forth past Kelin and Talas, scorching the ground and air behind them. Screams were short lived as many were incinerated on contact. Ganna knew instantly that their race was about to be extinct. She coordinated with other council members to rescue as many as they could while she opened alternate gates with random destinations. Anywhere was better than what would now be a dead planet.

Chardon rushed to the console to try and close it.

Too late.

He felt his core ripped out of him as his body was sucked into the vortex. Jaron tried to reach for him but the same happened to her along with Talas and Kelin. The last thing they saw before their souls died was the bomb going off in the distance, scorching the entire planet black.

Truth Sets You Free

Chardon thought by hearing the truth he would be more objective. He was wrong. His heart raced with an emotion of hate, despair and shame all rolled into one. He knew the one responsible for it all was his mate, Sestis. Talas and Kelin were just pawns.

"How stupid can you be?" Jaron had come back to hear the confession. "You thought the two of you could RULE over us?" She moved to strike. Modas stopped her, shaking his head. It was not worth it anymore.

"I..," Kelin began to say.

"Don't." Chardon raised one hand up. "Loving someone doesn't mean following them blindly. You should have had the common sense to deter Talas from such deceit."

"I understand."

"Do you, Kelin? No matter, what's done is done." He got up from his sitting position on the floor and made eye contact with everyone in the room. "None of this leaves here! The last thing we need is our people hearing that Sestis had a hand in this."

He left as did the rest of the cabinet members, leaving Talas and Kelin alone to think about what they wanted to do next. Atonement was not going to be easy.

Chardon paced the length of his chamber, doubt welling up about how to deal with the two. Somewhere deep in his core, he knew that he was in some degree to blame for their actions. His race would have been enslaved, probably, and the death toll, although intolerable would have been minimal. Most of their race would be alive instead of nearly extinct. He had been unwilling to submit to Halfar under any circumstance and this was the result.

Back then, Sestis acted like a tyrant when she visited other worlds to establish their place among the galaxy, spouting her own agenda without asking anyone's opinion. His passive aggressive, power hungry mate never turned away from new ideals because it kept her in high standing with the other councils. It should have been obvious what kind of manipulative female she was, yet he was blinded by some sense of accomplishment. It fell apart when he met Halfar at one of the interplanetary conferences.

How could I have let all this happen?

He looked out the window when it came into view as he slowed his pacing to a stop. Children played as if nothing was wrong. Workers tended the fields in silence with small smiles on their faces. That weak, dull sunlight muted the planet's colors. Some of the people's eyes were beginning to change in compensation for it. This was not how it should be.

He laid his palms flat against the walls on either side of the window shifting his weight to them. So much damage had been done. Even if Talas and Kelin had not betrayed their race, he believed the outcome would be no different. Chardon was not willing to condemn the pawns for the sake of the leader's reputation.

Eyes a dull bluish grey, the color of a dark, cold, churning sea reflected back at him through the window pane. On Earth, his eyes were a dark blue and even then, they seemed cold. He let out a deep sigh, hanging his head for a moment before pushing off the wall to stand straight. This time he would make better choices and right now, he needed to find a way to fix this planet for longevity. They would no longer run from their enemies.

Modas silently stood behind Chardon who jumped with fright as he turned to leave, nearly running into him. Such stealth in someone so massive still seemed to amaze him.

"Modas, please refrain from entering my chamber without permission."

"My apologies. I felt it would be better to come unannounced to clarify what you intend to do about those two."

"Absolutely nothing."

"Not even an apology?"

Chardon begin to shake a little.

"I can't do that."

"Why not?"

"Because then they would ask me why!" Tears started to form in his eyes. He refused to let even one drop. "I will make it right in my own way."

"You can't make it right, Chardon, and you can't keep secrets forever."

Modas stepped aside so Chardon could flee out of the room before him. He was the only other one who knew the reason for what happened thus far and would keep it to himself as long as Chardon wished. There was no need to cause more chaos and distrust among their race. He headed back to Talas' temporary chamber to break the good news that all was forgiven.

Unlike Chardon, he held the two of them responsible for the simple fact that they opened the gate. Chardon may have wounded Halfar's ego, the outcome possibly the same. There was no way that planet bomb would have succeeded without a doorway to go through. For Modas,

Chardon's conscience was clean, Talas and Kelin's were not. He knew Jaron felt the same way.

Talas jumped up from the bed with an expression of joy. "Really? We are forgiven?"

"According to Chardon, yes. You can both regain your status as cabinet members."

"But not by you." Kelin could see it in his eyes.

"No." Modas left the room.

Talas was left standing with an awkward half opened smile on his face. He closed his mouth and sat back down. It occurred to him that would be the case. Their race needed them, Jaron and Modas begged to differ. Most of their children were dead: no cores or vessels remained.

"Kelin."

"There is nothing we can say or do to make this right. We need to come up with a plan to get this planet right for our race and find a way to defeat Halfar because he will not stop at Earth for conquest. He knows we have a new home and if he is still angry, he will come after us out of spite."

"I'm not so sure." Talas leaned toward Kelin. "Did it seem odd to you that Halfar was not too interested in the bloody mess going on in that throne room?" Kelin thought back on it. "I think he wants to get the whole conquest over with, leave it to his generals and abdicate."

Jaron returned after cooling off followed by Ganna, Modas and the other council members.

"We could use that to our advantages." Kelin had ideas swirling in his head.

"That 'we' better mean the entire council and not the two of you doing something stupid on your own, resulting again in the destruction of our race." Jaron came into the room slamming the door open with such force the bang echoed throughout the compound, making them both jump back in fear.

"Of course not," Talas mumbled under his breath.

"What could be at our advantage?"

Kelin explained the killing ritual they witness in the throne room. They all listened, their stomachs made ill. He left nothing out because he wanted them to know just how frightful a creature Halfar really was.

"Disgusting. That is their idea of entertainment?" One of the councilmen shivered.

"If he is so detached then it may be possible to actually negotiate with that monster." Jaron rested one elbow in the hand of his other arm and tapped his fingers to his lips. "We first need to know what it is he seeks."

"Chardon," Modas blurted out at the same time the man himself entered the room. No one realized his blunder except Chardon and his eyes narrowed at him.

"Yes, I am here." Chardon used the opportunity to shy them away from it.

"I wish there was a way to sneak onto Earth and take them all out quietly, but he can sense a vortex opening anywhere in close proximity."

"The problem is those enforcers are kept partially evolved therefore they have no real mind of their own. Whatever their leader orders they obey." Chardon could still feel the wounds that were no longer there. "To stop the enforcers, we must first stop Rass and Kur."

That was an unpleasant thought for everyone in the room. Hideous creatures, the both of them, in their true forms and deadly. Maybe more so than Modas in close combat. Nothing, short of tearing them apart, would suffice as victory.

"No way do we get to Halfar without doing that. How many warriors can we have within the next two to three

Earth years?" Talas knew it was a short timeline.

"With our dwindled population, possibly two hundred," another female council member calculated.

"That's plenty."

Kelin was shocked by the number. He was expecting somewhere around Fifty.

Chardon looked up at the ceiling contemplating something. All eyes were on him. When he looked back down at them he made a proposal.

"We send only fifty to Earth and the rest will stay to defend this planet if necessary. The fifty will be split into four squadrons surrounding Halfar's palace from all sides."

"That's an odd number for a four-corner enclosure."

"No, it's not. Ten for each squadron and we will go into the main entrance to confront Halfar."

"We?" Jaron tilted her head.

"You, Modas, seven warriors and I."

"Do you think that wise?" Ganna interjected.

"It was started with Halfar and I, so it must end that way as well."

And the four squad leaders?" Kelin was curious, feeling it in his gut.

"Jaron, Talas, Ganna, and you."

The rest of the council's heads bobbed collectively in agreement. Better this way than the recruitment of council members with no combat experience. They would stay on the planet and oversee everyday expectations. Bloodshed was not their forte.

"We must go through the vessels that were saved and see how many match the cores in the garden. All the ones that do not have one or the other should be made compatible to ensure every core and vessel is consumed. From there, we can have a more accurate population count."

Ganna did not like that last suggestion. Forcing a core into a vessel not naturally its own could be dangerous. At the same time, having empty vessels and homeless cores was not an option either. "I will oversee that myself until it is time for deployment to Earth. Come," she gestured to the other council members.

"Modas." The tone of Chardon's voice was a warning and a beckon.

Modas went to his side.

Kelin and Talas sat back watching Modas and Chardon whisper to each other while Jaron, still elbow in hand, paced staring unwavering at them. Kelin saw the cold rage in her eyes as her gaze fell on Kelin and deepened as she caught Talas'. She had every right to wish them dead, so he did not flinch this time and neither did Talas. It was clear that if she had the means to murder them without the wrath of Chardon coming down on her, she would do it.

"Jaron, let's go." Modas was done talking with Chardon and they both waited for her to leave with them. She hesitated at first. "We have work to do." Modas insisted.

As the room cleared once again, Talas let out a deep breath releasing tension. Kelin seemed perplexed. They were both silent for a long time, Talas broke it.

"What are you thinking about, my love?"

Kelin glanced sideways at him. The "my love" sounded condescending at best. He chewed his lower lip. Something was amiss.

"What do you think Chardon and Modas were discussing earlier?"

"Who knows," Talas shrugged, laying his head on Kelin's shoulder. "I think it had something to do with Halfar."

"Mmm." Talas was falling asleep.

Kelin remembered what Chardon said about all of it starting with him and Halfar. It hit him as he also remembered Modas saying Chardon's name when no one knew he had entered the room yet. Could it really be that Halfar wants Chardon? Why? What were the terms of the negotiations that the council was not privy to? All these questions were going to get answered one way or another, he counted on it.

Talas was asleep on his shoulder and for the first time since they were made whole again by their cores, he stared at his sleeping face. Talas was never beautiful as Sara. Now he was a stunning sight to behold. How he must have hated being unintelligent and weak minded as a female earthling. Kelin put his arms around him and pulled him closer to breathe in Talas' natural scent.

It wasn't that Halfar didn't like conquering worlds, he just found Earth to be banal. Humans were so easily manipulated by power and greed they forgot to assume their enemies end game. For now, Halfar gave them power to attain status and money but, that would all be for naught once his armada moved in. The ones who defied him were smart to rebel. He smiled a little before frowning.

Kur had, yet again, crept into the throne room unannounced to catch him in an un-ruler like mood and started to get annoying.

"Does that smile preclude good news on our timeline?" Kur asked.

"It does. In another two years, we will be able to lock down this continent and move into the next. I look forward to getting off this world and on to more challenging ones."

"Granted, there are no unforeseen complications with this invasion."

"What could possibly go wrong?" Halfar raised his eyebrows.

"I believe there is a race that is not too happy to be nearly extinct because of you."

"They do not have enough warriors or destructive power to challenge us."

"Many battles have been won by sheer determination against foes bigger than us. Be careful, my lord, not to let your guard down."

"That is what my generals are for." Halfar glared at him.

Kur let out a smirk. He knew all too well what his role was in Halfar's armada. Leaving, he strode past Rass as he entered the throne room. Halfar watched them give each other hateful smiles of acknowledgment. Soon, he would appoint one of them to be in control of his Armada. It was just a matter of who and how.

Modas slid onto the bed, hovering over Jaron as she slept on her side. He listened to the even breathing escaping her partially opened lips. How beautiful she was laying there unsuspecting of his intentions at this very moment. He pulled the covers off her in one stroke, startling her out of sleep. Jaron curled upwards glaring at him in distaste for waking her in such a manner. He didn't care about that. Grabbing her by an ankle, he pulled her flat below him.

"Stop it, you beast! Let me go!" Jaron tried sitting up to strike him, missing as her center of gravity was off and she landed flat on her back again.

"No." Was all Modas replied as he used one hand to remove her robe and the other held both ankles down.

It usually happened this way: Jaron protesting half-heartedly and Modas being passive aggressive. He moved closer towards her so that the weight of his lower body held hers in place and removed his robes. For one brief instant, Jaron stopped fighting to gaze at his massive muscular body. She was tempted to reach out and touch him, restraining herself. It was too late, he saw the look in her eyes and with one movement pulled her legs through his and spread them around his waist.

"Stop!"

Jaron swung at him, her wrist caught in midair to be repositioned above her head.

He entered her roughly, his weight bearing down, forcing her legs open wider. They were now eye to eye and he did not disconnect his gaze even as she turned her head to the side trying to bear the pain and ecstasy without him knowing. To be this close and connected to her was almost too much for him. He could not and would not stop until he had his fill of her. He grabbed her by the back of her neck and turned her to him, kissing her hard. She finally submitted to him and buried her fingers deep into his thick mane, returning his kiss.

The sun had not yet set.

Ganna had followed Modas to discuss battle plans. She stopped outside of the bed chamber door when she realized he did not notice her. He had another agenda on his mind. She heard sounds of mating coming from inside and lingered a bit before leaving. It did not surprise her that they would produce a litter so soon after returning. Ganna smiled.

If it were up to Chardon, he would create new vessels and start over, knowing that option was a last resort. For now, the matching of core to vessel would take precedence to ensure a pure race. The process would take nearly a year to complete and, after that, preparations for the attack on Halfar would begin. Just seeing the garden made him feel helpless and guilty.

A small gust of wind blew his ever-growing hair, now almost to the middle of his back, with slight waves, into his face. He remembered it being as long before their world was destroyed.

Running his fingers through his hair, an image flash before him from long ago. Halfar in full regalia standing in front of him with his hand tangled in Chardon's hair against the backdrop of an aqua green sky.

Chardon knelt next to a row of cores, staring into the soil, mesmerized. It should not have happened this way. He could still see the look of longing on Halfar's face, his strange murky green eyes narrowed in frustration. Not wanting to recall those moments, Chardon shook his head in defiance. This was not the time for that. He stood and sensed Ganna getting closer to his location.

"Taking a short reprieve from the council?"

Ganna side stepped a garden slug under her feet.

"It has gotten cooler. The air feels nice."

"Hmm, you seemed far away a moment ago."

"Just, thinking about the past. Did you get to talk with Modas?"

Ganna's cheeks flushed and Chardon raised his eyebrows questioning.

"He is preoccupied with mating right now."

"Oh." Chardon was a bit taken aback.

He had not expected them to do that so soon. "I guess it can't be help. Even though they were always together on Earth, it is much different now."

"I am surprised he waited as long as he did. How frustrated he must have felt."

"I almost feel bad for Jaron, forcing herself to try and resist his advances all the while enjoying every minute of it."

"She is so dishonest with herself. Why does she torment him so?"

A worker came up to them and bowed. "I double checked all the vessels and the recorded cores and, I apologize, your mate's core and vessel were one of the ones destroyed."

Chardon looked away, his eyes downcast with no feelings in them. He had known that was the case and never asked for anyone to find her. It was for the best anyway. He didn't love her to begin with; she was just a means to an end for companionship.

"Thank you, there is no need to apologize. Go, finish your work."

As the worker left, Ganna watched Chardon shuffle his feet in the dirt.

"You couldn't care less about her being destroyed." She said so unceremoniously.

"I did care for her. Love her? No. If only you knew what kind of creature she really was."

"I do know. That is why I do not mourn her unlike our people." Ganna sighed.

Longing

Rass could see that Halfar was in no mood for entertainment this evening. His lord's facial expression was of someone far away in another land. He had an idea where, and who, he was thinking of. It was a bond not easily broken, apparently. He motioned his enforcers to drag away the carnage into an adjacent room to finish up and stepped closer to the throne in ear shot of Halfar.

"Does the sun not shine on your precious planet?"

Without noticing who was asking, Halfar answered. "It shines no more since the planet is now dead." He blinked hearing his own voice and seeing Rass so close to him.

"As I thought, you still want Chardon back. What is it about that inferior species you can't seem to break from?"

"You would not understand if I explained it." "Explain what, my lord?"

Kur slowly waltzed into the room, his long sword swinging in its holster behind him causing his cape to flow out. He might have passed for beautiful if his smile was not so menacing, and sent people running in terror because they knew what it communicated.

"Good of you to check in, General Kur."

Rass was taunting him into a fight to steer from the conversation. For Kur to know any more than he already did, which was plenty, would not be in Halfar's best interest.

Kur was not fooled, deciding to play the game.

"I always make sure our ruler is up to date on my success. Tell me, how many sectors have you claimed this week?" He smiled.

Two grunt workers came in to report an uprising in one of Rass' sectors, making him curse and hurry out of the room. Kur watched him go, a look of pleasure that his little prank had come to fruition, then turned to Halfar. That faraway look had returned, and Kur did not like it.

"So, my lord, what is it that needs explaining? Does it pertain to our campaign?"

"No, it does not. You need not know."

Halfar rose from his throne and exited to his private chamber. Kur's curiosity rattled him. He needed some time to think.

In his bed chamber, Halfar laid down closing his eyes. He drifted off to a memory long ago when Chardon traveled to different worlds gathering information as he had. They were collecting data on new technologies and other resources that could benefit their race. Some of the other rulers tried getting what they needed through manipulation.

Halfar was ruthless and blunt where Chardon tried the honest approach, although he was constantly undermined by Sestis. She has just as manipulative as the others, only with a superficial sweet nature. On those off days where no trade negotiations commenced, Chardon and Halfar talked.

Dreridian System long ago

"This world reeks."

Chardon covered his face with a sleeve in an effort to ward off the stench. He eyed the large metal structures spewing pollutants into the air only a few miles away. The landscape reminded him of some poor species' guts thrown onto it then coated with liquid metal. That was just about the right description of the smell Chardon tried to not breathe in. "It is an industrial planet." Halfar laughed. "Many different chemicals are produced here to make other products for distribution."

"It still reeks."

"How childish of you."

Halfar removed Chardon's hand from his face, lacing his fingers into his hair as he did so. A slight breeze came across the balcony where they stood. Their eyes locked on each other for a brief moment. The Aqua colored sky yielded to the sun tinting it with green, accenting his strange murky green eyes.

"Don't." Chardon whispered, his eyes never leaving Halfar's.

"I want you to rule with me."

"Please."

Halfar's eyes narrowed. He had been rejected before by others. From Chardon it was unbearable. He didn't know why there was no one in the universe he wanted more than Chardon. As if their life forces drew off each other.

"I won't give up."

He slid his hand out of Chardon's hair.

"I know, but, the answer is still no. I have a mate."

"Who you despise."

"I do not despise her, just her way of doing things."

"You don't love her."

Chardon severed the gaze. "It doesn't matter. Our people adore her."

"How?" Halfar jolted back.

That was incredulous to him.

"She is not like this on our world. Only when we are on other planets does she show this side of herself."

"All the more reason."

A soldier from his armada came up and whispered into his ear. Annoyance spread on his face. "I must go. Will I see you at the evening eating party?"

"Yes, my mate and I will be there."

"I didn't ask about her." Halfar turned and left Chardon alone on the balcony.

Halfar could still remember how soft and smooth Chardon's hair felt. He wondered why he thought of that day in particular and knew the instant after thinking it. Their minds were linked meaning Chardon had remembered as well not too long ago. Laying his hand on his chest he took a few deep breaths. Thinking of Chardon made his blood race.

Pregnancy made Jaron moodier than usual. Everyone, except Modas, steered clear of her. She had a tendency to hiss at anyone who came near her. Modas was not affected in any way by this. He still stole kisses from her and climbed atop her in the middle of the night, with her protesting at every turn.

Jaron could not fathom why she did all this. She loved her mate more than life and cared deeply for her race. Her emotions were all over the place and feeling heavy, carrying Modas' litter didn't help. There would be four, possibly five, little ones with either Modas' traits or hers.

The thought made her smile a little. She felt the presence of some children nearby and turned to give them an icy cold stare. They stopped dead in their tracks, eyes wide, then ran from her. That also made her smile in a mischievous way.

"You need more nourishment than that." Ganna stood beside her, pointing to the small bowl of raw fruits and vegetables on the ground by her feet.

"Yes, yes, I know that. This is just to hold me over until sunset meal." Jaron grabbed a fruit and took a big bite out of it, chewing noisily. "It's a good thing they are tiny little creatures because I could not haul them around like this feeding them constantly."

"You make it sound so unbearable." Ganna clucked at her. "Really, Jaron."

Swallowing a chewed-up chunk of fruit, Jaron replied, "I know." A look of sorrow replaced the frustration on her face. Why do I act this way and say things I don't mean?

From the other side of her, a plate of steaming meat simmering in its juices was laid next to the bowl of produce by Modas. He stepped away and sat down on the grass nearby, waiting for her to eat it. There would be no argument about it. Jaron used her fingers to tear apart a piece of meat and put it in her mouth.

"Well, I will let you enjoy that wonderful offering of nutrients from your beloved mate."

As Ganna walked away, Jaron slid a glare at Modas. He didn't register it. She sighed and continued to eat the meat along with the fruits and vegetables. Both sat in silence, neither moving from their positions.

"Why do you even put up with me?" Jaron asked with a mouth full of food.

"You mean everything to me."

Modas came forward and kissed her deeply. At the last moment, she turned, pulling away from him.

Immediately, she hated doing that. He could probably tell by the way she tried to act like nothing happened and continued to eat.

"See you at home."

Jaron gave birth to five little ones. Three were tiny balls of fur not yet ready to uncurl and open their eyes, and two were smooth skinned crying infants. She kept them close to her body for warmth, shooing Modas away whenever he came to try picking any of them up. Some days her level of territorialism was high, other times she would wave Modas away with them as if they were a bother.

As the little balls of fur uncurled, she could see their tiny noses, tightly shut eyelids and partial mouths. They resembled baby hedgehogs she had seen on Earth. Their fur ran from the top of their heads to their feet. Once they start growing, the fur would recede up to the middle of their spines.

Jaron wanted them to open their eyes to see what color they were. Usually, the entire litter was the same, though never a guarantee. She hoped they had Modas' eyes.

Chardon watched the workers carefully move the three vessels into the cryochamber and place the cores inside. Depending on how well the vessels could regenerate determined how long it would take for them to fully awaken. Two were badly mutilated and the other was partially scorched. It would take some time and he knew their cores were strong. Those three were necessary to revive in the first wave because he needed them as warriors.

Swiping his hand gently across the chambers, he whispered, "Your arrival will be a much-celebrated event, young ones." Chardon left the medical bay for sunset meal.

Tribulations

Government sectors fell instantly in the North American region. Kur's enforcers laid waste to entire districts as a warning to officials who dared defy Halfar. An invisible barrier had been erected that enclosed strategic areas of the continent for easy targeting. It was safe to assume that the next country would not fare well against Halfar's armada. He drug out the assault for the sake of entertaining his generals with new missions to conquer. Even they began to tire of them.

"Maybe we should just leave this place and send a planet destroyer," Rass stated.

He appeared to be up to the task.

"How tasteless." Kur shook his head in disgust. "That would not be dignified."

"Your aesthetics towards bloodshed are getting tiresome."

Both drew weapons with one hand and morphed the other arm into pincers. As the clashing of hard shells rang through the halls, Halfar ended it.

"Enough!" He was irritable at best and had no tolerance for their foolish taunting. "What are the reports from the inner city?"

Rass sheathed his weapon and bowed to him, his arm reverting to normal.

"The people outside of the district are unaware of the

chaos. Dealers are still making a profit, they just have no idea where the merchandise is coming from."

"Good. Let's keep it that way for the next few months."

"Are we not moving the timetable up?"

Kur seemed baffled.

"There is no rush."

Halfar assumed his usual lounging position on his throne. Kur glance at Rass who shrugged, and they went to dispatch more enforcers to a region three states over, per his previous instructions. At least they were being kept busy for now.

Modas reached into the sandbox to pick up the rowdy fur ball by its midsection. It tried to make itself into a ball again by curling around his hand. He carried it over to the climbing rock: a black monolith that reached towards the heavens, and planted it on the surface. Tiny claws came out to grab onto the rock.

"Now, use up that energy of yours with this." He watched the little one sniff at the rock and readjust its claws. "Go on." It inched upwards a bit, making a trill coo sound, then went a little more. "I will call you Trinon." His son turned towards him and cooed again in approval. Modas smiled. They were so much fun when that tiny.

"What are you doing?"

Jaron came screaming towards him.

"He was terrorizing his siblings."

"So you stick him on that giant monolith so he can get hurt?"

"He's not hurt." Trinon lost his grip and fell onto the ground with a high-pitched yelp. "Oh."

Modas saw blood on his tiny claws as Trinon mewed in pain, rolling around back and forth.

Jaron glared at him as she picked up her tiny son and held him close to her breast.

"Monster."

"Hmm." Modas checked the claws. "He will learn how to do it without falling."

"When he's older!"

"He's fine." Trinon was already struggling to get out of his mother's grasp.

"Did you name him?"

"Trinon."

She picked him up and held him high while he still squirmed. He could see her emotions going haywire again and knew she understood that Trinon would be protected like his siblings. The little one was feisty to say the least. She reluctantly handed him over and went back to tend to the others. Modas raised him in the air the same way she had done. Trinon liked it even less.

Modas brought all of the little ones to the fields so they could roll around as they pleased while he and Jaron kept watch. The weak sun was at its brightest time of day. The sound of them cooing made them both happy and they stared in awe. Sensing someone coming near their spot and they both looked out to see who it was.

And sat stunned.

A young manbeast in workers robes walked slowly towards the fields. He was nearly six feet seven inches tall with dark brown hair parted in the middle at the top and cascaded down his back. His full lips he inherited from his mother and his eyes, a deep shade of metallic silver, from his father.

As he got closer, seeing the shock on their faces, he realized Chardon had not informed them of his arrival.

"Well, I see you have replaced me with a new litter already." He laughed. Jaron and Modas did not. "I'm joking." Tears welled up in Jaron's eyes. "Please, don't do that."

Trinon rolled into his foot so he stooped down to pick him up by his midsection. He held him up high and grinned at the squinty eyed rebellious face.

"Mota." Was all Jaron could say.

"At least you remember my name." He set Trinon back down.

"That's not funny."

"Sorry." He went to her and hugged her tight. "I didn't think I would ever see you again."

"Nor I." Jaron cried into his chest. Her face showed hope that it wasn't a dream, glad it was not.

Modas stood with his hands clinched tight into fists. He did not know what to do or say. One of their children, known to be dead, was standing here in front of them. It was too much to bear. Mota looked over and grinned. Mota always had that face even in bad times. He took things in stride and not too seriously. When Jaron finally disengaged, Modas hugged him.

"My apologies for not telling you sooner." Chardon said loudly as he came up the hill to stand next to them and bowed humbly.

"You conniving…"

Modas stopped Jaron from advancing towards him, arm raised.

"I thought you would be happy." "That's not the point!"

"Isn't it?" Chardon stepped closer to her. Jaron lowered her arm. "Even you cannot be so heartless as to suggest he is not wanted."

"There is more. You need to tell them, Chardon," Mota said while taunting Trinon in the sandbox.

"Stop that!" Jaron commanded him. She turned to Chardon. "What else is there?"

"We were able to find two other vessels of your children. They are still regenerating. Mota seemed to recover faster than we hoped."

"Of course he did," Modas said matter of fact.

"I was a bit of a mess, though. My last memory was not pleasant."

"Speaking of which, I need to get you up to speed. Can you swear to no retaliation on your part?" Chardon was being serious now.

"Retaliate? Against who?" Mota snorted.

"Let's just say, your mother and father do not agree with my decision."

Mota glanced from mother to father, questioning them silently. Modas was aware how apparent their anger was regarding it.

"I can't say that, but I will hear what you have to say."

"Good, follow me."

Mota flicked Trinon's tiny nose hard and laughed when he mewed in pain. Toying with the little ones was a fun past time of his. The others rolled away or crawled from him. Trinon, on the other hand, was not backing down and Modas felt he would suffer for it.

"Mota!" Jaron went to soothe Trinon. "Sorry." He left the room with Chardon.

"Will he be just as angry as we are?" Jaron asked.

"Probably not." Modas knew his son well.

"I am trying to forgive them, but I will never forget."

"As it should be." He circled her waist from behind and kissed the back of her neck.

Mirrors fascinated Halfar. Humans were so vain to care about such things as clothing and appearances. There was only one rule for his race and many others: be presentable and wash when needed. In battle there was no time for primping to impress the enemy.

He stood staring at his reflection in front of the huge embellished oval mirror across from his bed. It occurred to him that his skin had darkened due to the intense sunlight on this planet and his hair had gotten longer with lighter streaks in it. All in all, he was more than presentable, even strikingly handsome as he heard some females say.

One who needed no help to look perfect was Chardon. Halfar thought of him more than usual lately. Perhaps due to the fact that he knew Chardon would come personally to stop his conquest of Earth. He looked forward to seeing him again as his true self, not Charles. That image of him on the balcony was replaced by a different memory.

He could hear water swishing in the chamber ahead and knew it was Chardon's. Nearing the door, he noticed it was ajar and entered without announcement. Chardon stood in female form, naked, dripping wet from the bath. Her hair flowed down the middle of her back, stuck to the skin. The slight curves of her body were silhouetted by the sunlight entering the solitary window on the left of the chamber.

Chardon's body went stiff and she turned her head around to see him standing there with lust in his eyes. She quickly went behind the changing curtain.

"What are you doing in here? Why are you not escorted?"

She threw on a dressing robe and came from behind the curtain; the thin robe clung in certain spots where her body was still wet.

"Your guards are lacking. It was quiet, so I came to find you." He moved further into the room until they stood inches from each other face to face. His hands ran across her breast then down. She slapped his hand away and he laughed. "But, you like that."

"I never said such a thing."

"You didn't have to."

Halfar extended a dark red talon that curved to widen in diameter. Sunlight made it glossy in appearance and it was quite smooth. Chardon did not move as he slid the talon underneath the drape and slowly inserted it into her. He watched her shudder.

"Submit to me."

Her stare glazed over, and he removed his talon, glistened with her juices, from inside. He watched her gaze shift to the wetness between her thighs and attempt to wipe it away, her hand stopping short.

"Don't." She pleaded.

He grabbed her face with both hands and kissed her passionately. She tried to push him away, fearful someone might come through the door he left ajar. Then she returned his advances in kind. They exchanged breaths for what seemed like an eternity until they heard movement down the hallway. She wrenched from him, a tiny tendril of saliva briefly connecting them.

"You need to go." Chardon went further into her chamber to change back into male form and dress in council robes.

Ganna and four manbeasts came into the chamber, surrounding him. He felt a smile form on his lips as one of the manbeasts gestured for him to vacate the room. Ganna seemed annoyed by his expression. As Halfar was escorted out, he turned to see Chardon come out to follow them as if nothing had happened, still somewhat damp.

And always beautiful, Halfar thought to himself.

He averted his gaze from the mirror, turning around to sit on the mantle below, letting his weight settle against it.

"Come quickly, I don't how much more I can endure."

"Is something so dire that it needs to be endured?" Kur's voice broke his thoughts.

He was standing in the doorway of Halfar's chamber and this disturbed Halfar greatly. Kur had never done such a thing without expressed permission.

"Why have you come through my hall and now stand at my chamber door?" His hostility was duly noticed.

"You were not in the throne room, so I felt concerned for your wellbeing."

"Do not condescend me!" Halfar pushed himself off the mantle blocking the doorway.

"I get the feeling you are not taking this conquest seriously, my lord." The last part was spat out.

"Are you questioning my strategy?"

"I am merely trying to figure out what it is that you hope to accomplish by stalling this." Kur stepped back into the hall. "What are you waiting for?"

"A resolution."

Halfar closed the double doors, not before seeing Kur's narrowed stare.

Severing the bond between Halfar and himself would have been ideal, if he knew how. At the same time, Chardon didn't want to break it. The current shared memories had become a nuisance, creeping up on them even though they were worlds apart. Halfar catching him off guard in his chamber was not something he wanted to think about right now while he sat with the council discussing battle strategies.

"Are you not satisfied with the plan, Chardon?"

A council member was staring at him in concern.

"Yes, it sounds fine. We just need to fine tune it so that the number of casualties is kept to a minimum. I would prefer none, if possible."

"There is no guarantee of that when it comes to battle, Chardon."

"I know. Find a way, regardless."

As the meeting adjourned he caught Modas' sight locked on him. He sighed heavily and tried to avoid any probing questions from the manbeast.

"Yes, I was thinking about Halfar. How many warriors will you have by the next moon?"

Modas noticed the quick change in topic and decided to wait to have his questions answered.

"It seems to be around twenty, give or take."

"Will Mota have his own to command?"

"That is the reason you revived him."

"That is not the only reason, Modas." Chardon was angry. To know that is what Modas and Jaron thought of his actions pained him. "I understand your hurt and wanted to alleviate it, even just a little."

"I know. I am sorry."

"If only things had been done differently."

"Do you think our race would have been saved if you had submitted to Halfar?"

"The way he was then, no. But, we would have had a fighting chance to turn the tables. We would've had a choice."

Mota sat on a tree stump lost in thought, not hearing or noticing his mother coming his way. She stopped a few feet away. He could feel the question coming from her body language. It was not that he wanted justice, or anything like it, he wanted peace. Causing such conflicts with their own race never made sense. On the battlefield was different.

"I understand why you are so angry, mother. That does not change what has occurred. We must move forward." He turned to make eye contact with her. "Please. Let it be."

His mother's hands balled into fists and she bit down on her lower lip, fighting back tears. He sensed her rage for his refusal to agree with her on the matter. Even though he was asking as her son to forgive he acknowledged that she could not do that, it was not justice in her mind.

"I am still here." Mota could read her body language. "Yes, only three of us survived. Are we not good enough?" Jaron's head snapped back, and her gaze went wide. "You know what I mean, mother."

Tears streamed down her face as she stood frozen. He regretted saying it and went to her, pulling her close to him. She did not return the gesture as he knew she wouldn't. He always wondered why she did not like showing affection, physical or otherwise.

Kelin slowly eased up out of bed so not to disturb Talas who was still sleeping. Cold air hit his naked body, making him shudder. The window had been left open all night and even though the morning sun shined, the room was cold. He was tempted to crawl back into bed and steal Talas' body heat for a few more moments. They were both exhausted from mating during the night, possibly overdoing it since their last time together. He leaned over towards Talas and kissed his cheek.

A knock on the chamber door made him realize that they had missed the council meeting.

"Stay a moment!" He called out as he grabbed his robes, dressing quickly.

Opening the door revealed Ganna looking moody.

"My apologies, Ganna. I overslept."

"Both of you?" She was a little testy indeed.

From the bed, Talas rose to sit on his knees, his back to them. "What time is it?"

His speech was slurred from sleep. His pale, bare skin flushed with heat from being under the covers and his hair a tangled mess.

Ganna grimaced at the sight. She did not have the same admiration for their mating as she did Modas and Jaron. He resented the fact that something about the two of them copulating made her skin crawl. Even when Talas was in female form, which was rare, it seemed to irk Ganna. Talas was stunningly pretty with an air about him that reeked of dishonesty.

"Chardon would like you both to come to his chamber for a briefing since the council was not important enough for the two of you to attend."

"Mmm." Talas's back arched letting his hair brush across the bed covers behind him. He turned his head sideways towards her. "Is that a hint of sarcasm?"

"If you would please make it there at your earliest convenience."

"I feel good." He shook his hair out, sighing. "Thank you, my love."

Kelin blushed with embarrassment as he saw Ganna get angry and storm out of the room.

"Why do you torment her like that?" He went over to the bed and stroked his spine. Talas leaned further back and kissed him. "You really are such a menace."

"But you love me all the same." Talas stretched forward like a cat and moaned looking over his shoulder. "We should go before lord Chardon finds us uncooperative."

"Don't do that. We are indebted to him for letting us

stay on this planet with what is left of our race. You know, the one we betrayed for nonexistent glory."

"Yes, yes. I am eternally grateful." Kelin raised an eyebrow. "Truly."

"Get dressed. I'll wait for you."

"No bath first?" Talas pouted.

"No time."

He pulled Talas off the bed and dragged him off to behind the changing curtain.

Chardon folded his arms in front of him, a gesture he learned while on Earth to make him look more important, or so he thought. Talas and Kelin poured over the plans with such intensity that Chardon was almost impressed. Thinking about why their race had to go through this in the first place because of them, squashed that sentiment.

"So, you want us to be separate from each other during this little insurgence."

Talas looked up from the hologram plans on the table. Chardon did not fully trust them yet and his strategy said as much.

"You each have unique talents that would be beneficial on different fronts as opposed to in one sector. This is not punishment as you think."

"Halfar will be waiting," Kelin stated. "The throne room is such an open space. There's nowhere to hide if a fight breaks out. Are you sure going straight in is a good idea?"

"He may be waiting. His minions would never suspect it."

"How bold, and almost insane, of you, Chardon." Talas was not in agreement.

"I will not cower in fear of him."

"Yes, except marching in for a fight is not very delicate."

"You sound like Kur." Kelin said incredulous.

"Well, we do have certain aesthetics in common. I will acknowledge that."

"I'll have Mota back you up near the side of the palace," Chardon announced.

"Charming," Talas rolled his eyes.

"Talas!" Kelin winced as he yelled it.

Chardon undid his arms and watched them argue for a bit. They did work like a well-oiled machine together. There lay the problem; they influenced the other's judgment too easily. Keeping them separate during the battle was Ganna's intuition and Chardon had to concur.

"Enough." He didn't yell and was just as effective. "I will trust you as much as you trust in me." Chardon got up to leave.

"What if we don't?" Talas was only being hypothetical. He still didn't like it.

"Then we have a problem, don't we?"

"We do trust you, Chardon. Talas is just being, well, Talas." Kelin shrugged.

"It's not funny." Chardon left.

Kelin shook his head at Talas.

"Again, why?"

There was no reason for it, the way he antagonized Chardon by throwing distrust around.

"I wanted to see how far he would let it go. Relax, he knows I was kidding." Kelin's face said he wasn't so sure. "That frontal assault still bothers me. We know that throne room and even with Modas with him, it will get more than a little hairy." Kelin raised an eyebrow. "No pun intended."

"You were on Earth too long. A pun, really?" Kelin settled back down to scan the hologram again. "You're right though. It is a bold maneuver. So bold that it makes me wonder if Chardon has an ulterior motive."

"Your theory again?"

"Something about the negotiations did not sit well with me after the fact. To destroy an entire world and its race on a whim because its leader would not submit is extreme. Chardon is hiding something and Modas knows what it is."

Jaron could not believe her daughter, Mara, lay in a cryochamber almost completely regenerated. Her body, previously scorched black on the entire right side, now lay sleeping with new skin. She watched her bare bosom heave up and down as she breathed, wishing she could reach into the chamber and feel the warmth of her body. Her daughter's light brown hair was splayed around her head like a giant fan, her long body lean with muscle. She was two inches shy Mota's height. The air from her partially opened pink lips fogged the glass.

On the opposite side was her eldest son's vessel also in a cryochamber. She couldn't bear to watch his regeneration. His body had been blown apart, so the medics arranged the pieces as best they could to resemble a full body. The regeneration was nearly complete with only a few body parts needing to reattach themselves. As his mother it especially hurt to see.

Mota strode in with Trinon wrapped around an arm, the little one's tiny teeth embedded in his forearm. It was obviously in retaliation for whatever torture Mota had subjected him to.

"Is my sister not ready to grace us with her presence?"

He reached over his mother and rapped the glass. Trinon disengaged for a moment to view his older sister then resumed trying to inflict pain on Mota who just laughed at him.

"What have you done to him?" She pulled Trinon off Mota's arm. "And don't hit the chamber!"

"I'm sure she doesn't mind." He glanced over at Trinon. "He's just sensitive. I didn't do anything that I haven't done already."

"That's the problem."

"He's getting bigger, you know. You can't treat him like a baby beast much longer."

Jaron held Trinon to her and he immediately found his way into her robes and latched on a breast to feed, his tiny claws just barely sinking into her flesh.

"He's a little greedy, too," Mota laughed.

Jaron rolled her eyes at him. "So were you." She saw even Trinon gave him a woeful look between suckling. "Why just him?"

Mota stood up straight still staring down at his sister.

"Because, he's stronger than you think."

He walked off and yelled over his shoulder, "Tell the lazy one to wake up already."

Jaron sighed and tickled Trinon behind his ear. He did have a strong grip, maybe too strong. In another year he will be walking and trying to climb that behemoth of a mountainside. She was amazed that it had also been transported from their home world.

Looking down on Trinon, she knew he would need training to curb that urge to outdo everyone. She remembered assisting with her daughter's training and how the poor girl tried too hard by conjuring up energy to impress the elders.

The smell of sea water and beast invaded her senses. Modas had been meditating by the waterfall earlier and must have just finished. He was damp from misty spray that made the outline of his body shimmer in the sunlight. Jaron felt the pull of lust. She refrained from showing it even a little by glowering at him. As usual, Modas was not convinced.

"Finally came to see how your children are doing?"

"We have more than three now," was all he said.

"If it were up to you, we would have four or five litters running around."

"We'll have another soon enough."

"What makes you think I would have another litter with you?"

Jaron tried to sound angry. It came out in a quivering voice and she cursed herself. Modas did not answer.

Instead, he went over to the other side to check on their eldest still regenerating. It didn't bother him at all to see his son like that. Jakar was just as strong as his father so she assumed that's why Modas had no worries. A small chunk of flesh merged into a body part near the ribcage and healed the skin, leaving no marks. It was only a matter of time before he awakened.

Trinon's soft mewing could be heard throughout the room and Modas swung around in his seat just in time to see Trinon falling asleep in Jaron's arms. In those few moments, Jaron became filled with love and affection. Of the five, he was the fussiest, angriest, most sensitive and the strongest. Jaron knew Modas was playing favorites and had great plans for that one. Unlike, Mota, who was just tormenting the little one, he was going to train him properly.

Feeling her mate's stare, she tensed up. She had let her guard down. It was so easy to do when she was nursing one of their young. With not much fanfare, she wiped the excess milk off the breast Trinon had been suckling as if disgusted and covered herself back up. Looking up, she saw a wall of fabric as Modas leaned down to kiss the top of her head softly.

She did not even hear him move from across the room.

"You should rest." He could somehow always tell when she was tired.

"I will." Jaron began to stand, faltering from fatigue. "I guess I need a little help."

She did not fight him. He picked her up while she still held the sleeping Trinon and carried her to their chamber.

So many, Chardon spoke in his head as he combed the memorial site for the dead.

Whole families had been annihilated with no one to remember them, making the count inaccurate. Out of the corner of his vision he spotted Modas carrying Jaron to their housing. The one thing Chardon regretted most was that someone knew his secrets. He wished they had been buried in the memorial with all the other lost souls.

"I'm so sorry," he whispered to the dead.

"Why should you be sorry?" Kelin startled him. "There was nothing you could have done to prevent such a tragedy."

"True, but I like to think that I could have in some way."

Chardon's expression changed, and he realized too late it was a mistake to let Kelin notice. By the way Kelin stared at him he was probably thinking yes, maybe it could have been prevented regardless of their foolish stunt opening the gate.

"Whatever Halfar promised was all lies. You were right not to submit to his demands. We would all be slaves right now."

"Maybe."

Chardon turned and walked away from the memorial grounds.

☼

Rass was already walking faster than normal to keep up with Halfar who nearly sped down the hall to the battle room where Kur was waiting for him. The large entourage also struggled with Halfar's pace. He could tell just how angry his lordship was by the exposed, half formed, exoskeleton sections protruding from his skin. He had to do something, quickly.

"My lord!"

"I will not be made a mockery of by my own subordinates!"

"My lord!" Halfar was about to turn the corner that led to the battle room's hallway. "Stop!"

Everyone in the entourage halted; the enforcers stunned, Halfar incredulous. He turned slowly and walked back to where Rass stood in the middle of the hall.

"Did you just command me to stop?" Halfar had one arm formed into a claw.

"Please, my lord, come walk with me." Something in the way he said it made Halfar pause. "I need you to listen to me right now before you go in there."

"Everyone stand and wait," he ordered and walked with Rass.

"I know how frustrated you are with Kur and his solo antics, but that is what he wants. The more riled up you get the better his case to eliminate you. I know why you are stalling and I wish you success."

"Do you?" Halfar stopped walking and face him. "My success would mean leaving the Armada behind to live on whatever world she is in."

"Conquering Earth was not your idea, it was Kur's and now not even he wants to be on this wretched rock. The invasion will grind to a halt and then we leave."

"So, if I were to storm into the battle room in a rage."

"Kur would have his enforcers cut you down without so much as a witness to his treachery. It would be…glorious. His words, not mine."

"Then what would you have me do?"

"I can handle Kur. You just need to focus on your agenda."

Halfar relented and slapped a hand on Rass' shoulder.

"Even if I give you the reigns of the armada, he would fight you to the death for it."

"And I will make sure that I win so you can return our race to its true calling."

"You loved him once."

"He loves himself more than he ever loved me."

"Now what?"

Halfar removed his hand and there they stood alone with no guards while Kur waited for a fight to come to him.

"You go to your chamber and I will inform Kur of your displeasure."

"Can you really defeat him?"

"You, more than anyone, know the power I keep hidden."

"That is not what I mean, Rass."

He probed his face for acknowledgement.

"I know. Yes, I can, if it is the only way to stop him from pitching our race into ruin." He headed towards the battle room. "Go, my lord." He bowed deeply mid stride and continued on.

Halfar began to realize just how deadly the situation had become. Kur was now the enemy and there was no letting his guard down for a second. It always bothered him that Kur was near whenever he didn't want him to be. There was a way to avoid him and that meant going out into the streets incognito.

He knew Rass would help him with the logistics of it. "Well, Kur, let's see how well you fare against me."

A small troop arrived to escort him to his chamber hall. As they marched onward, Halfar had a vicious plan in store for Kur when the time came. No one defied him and got away with it. He slowed his walk as he thought about it and how that logic applied to Chardon. No, that was entirely different. His bond with Chardon was eternal, his connection to Kur was based on military might.

In his chamber, he stripped off his battle gear and robes to stand naked in the middle of the room. The cool air engulfed his body and he stretched upward. Crawling onto the bed, his thoughts drifted to Chardon on a faraway world he had yet to find.

Somewhere off in the distant fields, Kelin attempted to clear his mind, hunting small game with an archaic hand-made projectile weapon likened to a crossbow. Although the creatures on their new home were a bit strange, the meat was somewhat similar in taste to what he was used to. Keeping his thoughts away from the topic of battle plans and Chardon was his goal for the day.

He saw something scurry on his right and swung the weapon towards the sound, releasing the metal rod. A soft squeal and a thump came right after. It was the fourth one today which was enough for Talas and himself. Each chamber had to fend for themselves food wise twice a moon cycle. Evening meal captured, Kelin headed back home.

Talas was waiting for him as he entered the chamber. His long dirty blonde hair was slightly wavy from being damp after bathing without Kelin. He sat cross legged on the bed with a hologram of the revised battle plans in front of him. The look on Talas' face made Kelin want to turn around and go back into the fields.

"This is not looking like an easy exit for our little groups," Talas blurted.

"Please. I just want a quiet evening with you and not talk about any of this or Chardon for that matter."

He plopped his kill on the kitchenette's cutting block.

"Why are you bringing up Chardon?"

Then he remembered. "Ahh, your theory."

"A bit more than a theory. I think Chardon feels far more responsible for what happened than we do. I just can't seem to figure it out and there is no way Modas will ever tell me what he knows."

"Modas," Talas climbed off the bed to stand by him, "will never tell you anything, let alone speak to you unless it was necessary."

"I know."

"Then let it run its course. You will find out what is really going on, soon."

"Yet, I get the feeling you already know what's going on. Why are you feigning ignorance?"

"Because there is no point. And I know you would rather find out on your own as opposed to me just laying it out for you."

"True. I still think you could at least give me a hint."

Talas eyed Kelin's bundle of dead meat and smirked.

"And what are we having with that?"

"That is your duty, I hunted them."

"I don't think hunt is the word for such tiny creatures."

Kelin washed his hands in the basin behind the changing curtain then flopped down on the bed exhausted. The topper molded around his body and he started to drift off into sleep when Talas whacked him on the thigh.

"You're filthy! Go bathe at least!"

He forcibly pushed Kelin out of the bed. They both laughed.

A loud screech filled Jaron and Modas' chamber, forcing them to wake from their midday slumber and run to the sandbox that housed the little ones. One of the male baby beasts, Und, had Trinon by the face with his tiny claws and a look of frustration. The screech had come from him as a battle cry. Trinon had Und by the mane, refusing to let go until his opponent yielded.

"Stop that!"

Jaron could not believe the scene before her. The others just laid there in the sandbox watching with disinterest like this was an everyday ordeal, and it was to some degree. Modas had stopped at the edge of the sandbox and knelt. He too had the same look. She reached in and tried to disengage them.

"Let go this instant!"

Mota came from behind her, flicked both of them hard on the head and drew Trinon out. The little ones wailed loudly, tears and blood on their faces. It was clear who the aggressor had been. Trinon wiggled all over the place in an effort to get out of Mota's clutches without success. When Mota turned him over, Trinon bit into the meat of his bicep. It didn't hurt him in the least.

"Why is this happening?" Jaron demanded of Mota, knowing he was to blame. "And why are you doing nothing?" This was directed at Modas who just glanced up at her.

"Have you forgotten what it was like when I was a baby beast?" Mota smiled.

"That is not the issue!"

Modas picked up Und by the back of his mane and

turned him so they were nose to nose. Und stopped crying and mewed at him.

"Good." He set his son back down in the sandbox with his other siblings. "He's a fighter."

Jaron was on the verge of imploding with rage. She leaned over towards Modas and slapped him in the back of his head then turned on Mota, doing the same. They both were stunned into submission as she stormed out.

"Father, I believe we must start training them sooner than later. Mother is not about to tolerate much more disobedience." Modas nodded in agreement, holding the back of his neck.

Halfar was not lounging lazily on his throne today as Kur had anticipated. The great ruler seemed to avoid him at all costs, always sending Rass to do his bidding. Kur made a grunting sound of disgust. Ever since he had rejected Rass' affections, his counterpart had become one of Halfar's lapdogs, confirming his initial thoughts about him. Wiping that out of his mind he focused on Halfar seated on his throne looking as menacing as he once was, tapping a clawed finger on the arm rest.

"Are your enforcers in place?"

Kur nearly stepped backwards at the onslaught of the question.

"Almost, my lord." Halfar was not in the mood for games. "We are positioning a small team on their blind side to ensure coverage."

"That's good to hear. And?"

"My lord?" Kur was confused.

"Why have you come here? Surely it was not to report that you are in fact not ready? What other reason did you have to see me at this time of day?"

Kur had in fact come to irritate him for the pleasure of it. Since he had been called out on it, he was not too confident in doing so.

"I was worried since you had not been to the battle room in some time and sending Rass with your instructions."

"Is not Rass a General such as yourself?"

"Of course. I was not questioning your motives."

He bowed low.

"I shall take my leave to finish the preparations."

As he left cursing under his breath, he made a detour to the battle room.

"Well, that went smoothly."

Rass came out from behind the double doors of Halfar's hallway.

"I wanted to rip one of his limbs off."

"As you said, he is one of your Generals."

"Why is he, suddenly, so insubordinate? I don't understand."

"Simple. He is just as bored as you are and wants to engage in a real fight."

"A real fight means going against an unknown foe leading to casualties we cannot afford."

"Yes, that last battle saw our armada nearly cut in half. Luckily no one knows this, not even Kur." Rass' lip twitched into an almost sheepish smile.

"There is no reason for Kur to return to our home world and find out either. What is the status of our soldiers?"

"There are currently two thousand in the birthing tanks. This is the second batch and the third will be ready in under ten years." Halfar nodded. "It seems as you destroyed one world, our fate was sealed with the near destruction of your own."

Halfar stepped down from his throne to floor level.

"Which is why I want to make things right again. I wish you would stay with me when I find what world Chardon is on."

"I could not live with that race." Rass laughed.

"Why not?"

"I like things a bit messy."

"Hmm. You're right, it's not a good idea. The moment they open a vortex, trace it before closes. I need to be able to get there shortly after."

"As you command, my lord."

With a low bow Rass was gone. His boots echoed in the hall.

Mota carried Trinon by the mane swinging him lightly like a small sack as he strolled towards the giant rock monolith covered in claw marks from generations of manbeasts scaling it. As he neared it, he swung upwards towards the rock and released Trinon who went smack into it, his claws scrambling to grab a hold.

There were strange whimpering sounds along with the scraping of claws on stone then heavy breathing from tiny nostrils. Trinon had managed to secure himself on the monolith. Mota threw his head back and laughed so loud that some of the workers in the distance popped their heads up looking around for where it came from.

"That's not very nice, brother."

His sister, Mara, walked slowly down the hill. A tiny grin spread on her face. She was wearing a sleeveless grey robe over a long sleeved white one that flowed to the ground causing small whirlwinds.

"But look at him! It's amusing to see him struggle."

"You know, just because you were tormented as a baby

beast does not give you license to do the same with our little siblings."

"What do you know? You were not born a manbeast." He wagged his finger at her.

"That did not stop any of you from trying even though I am older than you."

"Not older than Jakar."

Mara frowned. Their older brother was not yet ready to be awakened. She had peeked into the cryochamber and nearly gasped in horror.

"He's almost complete, you know," she whispered.

"Why is everyone so sad? He's much stronger than any of us so let's not fool ourselves into thinking he will need some sort of pampering." Mota watched Trinon inch his way up.

"That's not what I meant! Mota, you exasperate me." She moved a lock of hair that the breeze had whipped into her eyes. "I would have said the same if it was you in there."

"I WAS in there, sister." He turned to her with softened eyes. "This was not supposed to be this way. I understand how you feel, I really do."

They hugged each other for a brief moment, disengaging when they heard a yelp followed by a thud. Trinon had fallen.

"He is adorable." She knelt next to him. "Look at that face!"

"I know, right?" Mota stood by her and they both watched Trinon wiggle to and fro on the ground until he came up on all fours. His eyes burned with anger and he shook his whole body to get rid of dirt imbedded in his fur. "I can't wait until he starts walking."

Modas stood nearby watching them torment Trinon and did nothing to alleviate him from their idea of entertainment. He couldn't wait either. Many plans went through Modas' head regarding the training he would have his children endure. He nodded his head and sighed.

Ganna couldn't stand to see anymore of Talas' amazing fighting skills. It irked her to no end that he was so good at battle, yet his personality reeked like a long dead animal carcass. What made it worse was that he smiled whenever he defeated an opponent.

"Narcissistic pig." She muttered under her breath the phrase she had learned during her stay on Earth.

"What was that, my sweet?"

Talas had not quite heard her, although he knew it was directed at him.

"I am not your sweet."

"No," Talas moved towards her, "you certainly are not."

"Stay away from me, you…"

Talas grinned. "Betrayer? Coward? Tell me what you think I am, Ganna." He swung his long sword with ease letting it stop short of her chest. She refused to play his game and left.

She heard his older sparring partner chastise him.

"You know, that behavior is not gaining you any points. We all wonder if you are capable of turning against us again."

"Let me make this clear, I will NEVER betray my kind again. That lesson has been learned in the harshest way." Talas returned to him. "Let's continue. I have a battle coming up in a years' time."

Ganna frowned.

I hope you get gutted like an animal, she cursed him.

THREE:

Secrets

Her body arched high above the bed as her hands dug deeper into herself. A sharp intake of breath was the result of her fingers finding that one spot inside, making her juices flow out to drip onto the bed coverings beneath her. Beads of sweat covered her entire body. She thrashed about for a split moment letting out a high-pitched noise. In her mind she was being so brutally violated yet could not stop herself from the ecstasy it gave her. She could feel his large member penetrating her without mercy.

"Chardon?" A female voice called from the doorway, muffled by the closed entry.

Her body froze, hands still deep between her thighs. She eased back down flat onto the bed.

"Are you awake? The council has called a meeting. I am here to escort you."

"Yes," Chardon managed to breathe out loudly. "Please stay a moment."

She flung the covers away and went behind the changing curtain to wipe herself down with water. There was no time for a bath. Taking a deep breath, she forced her body to shift back into male form.

Once complete, Chardon yanked on his council robes and stepped out into the room. He looked around to make sure there was no evidence and saw the bed drenched in sweat and other fluids he did not want to name. Throwing the covers back onto the bed to cover the mess, he headed out the door where his escort waited for him. He felt exhausted. Thinking of Halfar did that to him.

Halfar jolted from sleep, sitting up in a fog of images as he tried to slow down his heavy breathing. What he experienced, in what he thought was a dream, took most of the energy out of him. He remembered the last time he mated with Chardon and it was nothing so intense as that. It wasn't the fact that he could feel what Chardon was doing while she remembered. He could also see.

His bed was drenched, and knew Chardon's was even more so. If he found what world Chardon was on right now, he would go there and drag her by that soft hair of hers back to his palace to have his way with her for eternity. The entire ordeal was maddening, and there was no way he could think straight today; let alone command an army.

"Chardon, what are you trying to do to me?"

Wiping wet hair from his face, he got up.

☼

The cryochamber on the other end of the medical facility glowed softly as energy pulsed through it. Inside, Jakar slept soundly while his core integrated with his now fully regenerated body. Above him, Modas waited patiently for him to wake up. It had been so long since he talked to his eldest son and there was so much to tell.

A beep sounded, the cryochamber's locking mechanisms sprung and the canopy slid back filling the area with icy mist. As it cleared, Modas was able to see Jakar in his entirety. The muscles began to move and slowly, his eyes opened revealing the steely blues inherited from his father.

"How was your nap?"

Jakar glanced over at him and licked his lips. They were

severely cracked, and his dry tongue did nothing to cure them. Modas dipped a finger into the water basin next to him and lifted it over Jakar's mouth to let the moisture drip down. After a few drops, his son replied.

"I'm sure I was dead, so a nap is not correct." Jakar strained his muscles, forcing his upper body to sit upright. His long dark brown mane came up with him, the ends curving as they fell onto the chamber bed. "A robe would be nice." Modas grabbed the spare garments from the edge of the cryochamber and laid them on Jakar's lap. "Thank you, father."

Jakar swung his legs over the chamber's edge and stood. At six feet seven inches, he was only an inch shorter than Modas with just as much muscle only slightly leaner. He dressed in silence, making sure his hair did not get caught in the fabric of the outer robe.

"So, now you can tell me what happened."

"What do you remember?"

"Playing with Hon near the sandbox and then being blown to pieces. I do believe I watched one of my arms and a leg veer into separate directions before someone snatched my core out of me."

Modas' eyes darkened. "Sit." He told Jakar about Talas and Kelin, and their new planet. Jakar listened without speaking a word or asking any questions. When Modas was done, he got up and walked out.

Mara came rushing into the medical room only to find her father sitting alone.

"Where is he?" She asked.

"Walking."

"Why?"

"I explained everything to him."

Mara lowered her eyes. "That would make sense." She dragged a seat over to where he was and sat down next to him. "Was he angry?" Modas turned to her. "Of course he is, he just doesn't show it." Her head on her father's shoulder.

As great a fighter Talas was, he could never compare to a manbeast of Modas' descent. He watched a figure coming towards the sparring ring where he was showing off with some of the other warriors and as the person came closer he hissed in fear, recognizing Jakar. There was no expression on the manbeast's face which meant the same as when Modas looked that way: he was angry.

Jakar was still a good two hundred meters away as Talas tried to get around one of the men to make a break for it. It was too late as he witnessed Jakar move with lightning speed towards him, knocking his body backward twenty yards from where he had stood. Jakar now stood in the previous spot Talas had occupied on the sparring platform. He jumped down from it and walked slowly to Talas who had a hard time getting up. Talas raised his good arm from underneath him, the other its shoulder dislocated from the hit. Talking his way out of it was not going to work. He still wanted to try and reason with the overpowering Jakar whose claws extended.

"Please, I know that I can never atone for my mistakes! Don't…"

Jakar's talons went through his dislocated shoulder and part of his chest like liquid, the pain nothing so smooth. Talas let out half a scream before thinking better of it and clenched his teeth shut so hard, blood trickled from his mouth.

Jakar leaned in close to his face and whispered. "I won't kill you." He retracted the claws and stood, towering over Talas, malicious intent still in his eyes. "A reminder from me."

He walked away just as workers came running with medics. Talas watched Jakar head off into the fields. His vision started to blur as the manbeast got further away into the distance.

Kelin must have heard the ruckus going on near the sparring ring as did Ganna because both came rushing over to see the aftermath of Jakar's wrath. Kelin hurried to comfort him while Ganna examined the wound out of curiosity, nodding in approval of the mess. There was blood everywhere.

"Nicely done. The wound should heal perfectly but it will leave a scar."

Ganna had a smirk on her face that neither liked. Talas was awe struck when Kelin backhanded her with rage.

"You filthy…!" Kelin was about to stand when a hand clamped down on his shoulder.

"No need for more violence."

Chardon had arrived as well.

"I demand that he be locked in a room of solace!" Ganna shrieked, holding the side of her face. Her expression crumbled as Chardon's gaze bore down on her in disgust. Talas had never seen such a look from Chardon.

"Kelin," he redirected his eyes towards him, "go and make sure everything goes well with the medics."

As everyone dispersed, Chardon swung around to face Modas coming up the hill, in no hurry to explain, with Mara in tow. He watched their eyes follow the entourage of medics and soldiers helping Talas.

"Was my decree not clear?" He also glanced back at Ganna still on the ground.

"My apologies."

"That is not acceptable, Modas!"

Even Mara flinched from the hostility in Chardon's voice. Ganna crept further away from him.

Modas and Chardon stood face to face a few inches apart and a silent battle raged. Jaron, Mota and three council members stared at the six feet eight inches tall manbeast and their leader, who was just above six feet three, square off. Chardon's power was just as deadly as Modas' fighting skills.

"If my apology is not to your liking, we can accommodate." Modas dead panned.

"Will your children mourn you when I flay your corpse?"

Chardon's eyes did not waver.

Just as they stepped back into fighting stances, Jaron and Mara threw up an energy barrier between the two. The look of fright and horror on their faces made Modas and Chardon stop. Everywhere around them, people had halted their activities ready to run if necessary. Both men felt ashamed at their display.

"I am sorry, your apology is more than enough. I know Jakar does not forgive easily." Chardon stood tall.

"Understood."

Modas retracted his claws, straightening his stance.

Jakar came back after some thought and realized his error, witnessing the near showdown with his father and Chardon. His eyes widened with fear, then relaxed as his mother and sister put an end to it. All of this happened because he could not contain his temper. He saw Chardon, fist clenched in obvious frustration, leave the area and head towards the commons.

"My apologies, I didn't mean to cause such a mess."

He bowed to his father.

"No, it's fine."

"I…"

"You did what I wanted and could not." Jaron went to him. "Because of Chardon's decree to accept them back into our good graces, we are not allowed to touch them. You did not now this."

Jakar turned to his father. "So, I was not told everything?" Modas did not reply. "It was intentionally omitted in your recital."

"Father!" Mara spun on him. "That's irresponsible!"

"But," Mota slapped his older brother on the shoulder, "it was so worth it!" he laughed heartily.

Jakar felt a pull at the corners of his mouth.

"It did feel liberating. It was the first time I was able to use my claws since waking up."

They all laughed loudly for a moment then stopped, noticing Ganna was still there. She picked herself up feeling distraught. Seeing them, she understood her anger and meddling was petty compared to what they had gone through.

"Excuse me. I have to go check on Talas to make sure he is comfortable before surgery." Her steps were a bit unsteady, so she corrected her center of balance.

She could feel Jaron watch her with disdain. She knew the woman only tolerated her for her medical expertise, nothing more. After seeing and hearing what she had done, Jaron probably thought it served her right when Kelin knocked her around. There was no love lost between them. Ganna had lost no one important because she had always been alone. She liked it that way; sometimes.

A final backwards glance revealed Jaron stepping closer to her eldest son and craning her neck to look up at him.

"This can never happen again."

Like his father, all Jakar said was, "Understood."

Feeling lower than she had ever felt in her life, Ganna made her way through the crowd surrounding Talas in the medical chamber. She shooed everyone out except two medical assistants, even forcing Kelin to leave. She set herself next to the surgeon's table Talas had been placed on.

He was pale and shaking uncontrollably. His half-closed eyelids did not reflect pain. She knew how excruciating that wound must be and said nothing. He turned to her, his hair drenched in sweat, plastered against his cheeks. She gulped.

"Come to finish me off, my dear." His voice cracked a bit.

He licked his lips, tasting his own blood.

"No, Talas. I am first and foremost a surgeon."

"Really? You seemed to be entertained by my injuries." His body shuddered.

Ganna placed a hand on the bloodied arm bent against his side. "I apologize for that. It was wrong of me and I am ashamed. Now," she motioned an assistant to hand her the sealing tool. "This may hurt a bit since we are going to be forcing the wound closed. Are you ready?"

"Hah!" Talas took a deep breath. "You're going to have to do better than that to threaten me."

"Close the doors." She instructed the assistants.

As strong Talas may be, she guaranteed he would scream through the procedure. A wound from a manbeast was no easy fix. Even with the doors sealed Kelin, and the others, would still hear the muffled sounds of Talas screaming. Ganna forced herself to ignore it as it rang in her ears. She continued with the operation. It would definitely leave a scar.

☼

Down on the ground with his weight on the balls of his feet, Chardon planted his hands deep into the soil and retched until vomit spewed from his mouth. Knots had formed in his stomach from being so enraged, causing nausea. Spitting the last of it out, he let his hearing focus on distance and heard the muffled laughter of manbeasts along with Jaron and Mara. He felt played for a fool. His fists slammed into the dirt, ready to weep silently.

"It was bound to happen."

Kelin stood a few feet from him looking haggard, his sudden appearance cutting Chardon's self-pity short.

"Was I wrong to grant the two of you lenience?"

Chardon rose, brushing dirt off his robes then wiping left over vomit and spittle from his mouth. His eyes were bloodshot, so he didn't turn around. No one needed to see their leader in such a state.

"We are grateful for it. I fear the people may not have agreed with your decision."

"How is Talas?"

"Screaming his heart out while Ganna seals his wounds."

"I am sorry."

He frowned. It sounded like he was apologizing for more than just Talas. As if picking up on it, Kelin stepped closer.

"What exactly were the negotiations for back then?"

"Just like we had discussed." Chardon's eyes narrowed at the off-topic question, not liking the direct approach.

"You seem a little more than distraught about what happened. More so than Talas and I."

Chardon unclenched his fists and let out a heavy sigh. Keeping secrets was going to become more difficult as time went on. He was going to hold fast until there was no other alternative. Turning to face him, he moved a few steps away from Kelin to gain some distance and laid a hand on his shoulder.

"I am because as our race's leader, their lives were my responsibility, I failed everyone."

"You made a decision that you thought was right."

"And I was wrong. Possibly this time as well. I still stand by it."

"I need to go check on Talas."

Kelin went off to the medical chamber, leaving Chardon standing alone looking confused. He could tell Kelin knew he was dodging the question and it would confirm his suspicions even more.

Halfar had heard it explained before and still didn't understand why people spent their time at some random smorgasbord cluster of shops in the middle of nowhere. They called it convenience. Halfar had another less tasteful name for it. Chardon would agree.

Rass came out of what looked like an abandoned building which was in fact a safe house for local dealers whenever law enforcement decided to do a crackdown. It made Halfar laugh. He marched up to Halfar and came as close as possible, so he could whisper.

"Some government officials have sent spies into our territory and we caught them a few days ago. One of the spies was able to get a message out about the barrier before being dispatched immediately after. Needless to say, our time table has been moved up unexpectedly."

"How long before they can get someone to test the rumor?"

"I say in the next 48 hours. They can't just send reinforcements, there is a protocol to go through and this just happened about five hours ago." "Drop the barrier for seventy-two hours, starting now, just in case."

"As you command." Rass made a bow and left.

It had been awhile since he had been outside among

the humans and he remembered why he stayed in his throne room. The air on Earth reeked. He could never figure out where it came from being all over, in every country. Maybe a planet destroyer would do it some good and cleanse the whole ball of wretchedness.

On his left he saw a drunk couple stagger out of a bowling alley and into the clothing store next to it and an ice cream parlor. It was two in the afternoon. Halfar shook his head in disbelief along with the human patrons who bore witness. He officially hated strip malls.

As the battle date grew closer, everyone did their part to make sure all preparations were underway. The population was on the verge of tripling in such a short time and the workers had found a way for the planet's soil to yield more produce. All the willing volunteers of warrior age were trained daily and had improved considerably.

Mota watched with arms across his chest as Trinon, now a good four feet tall, clawed his way up the monolith determined to reach the top, which he was unable to do yet. The look a sheer will on his little face made Mota grin. He was a bit disappointed that Trinon was no longer small enough to be tossed against the wall anymore. He had found other ways to torment him. Their mother had another litter so new victims were imminent for next season. He could hear their little mews even from this distance.

Back to watching Trinon, he noticed his progress had taken him halfway up. That was too far up for him. If he fell all his bones would be broken, so Mota jumped from where he stood and landed a few inches above Trinon on the wall and snatched him off. He landed on the ground below in a soft thud with Trinon tucked under one arm screeching up an angry storm.

"Not so fast, little snotter." There was literally snot coming out of his nose. Calling him that only made him yell more. "Now, what would you have done if you fell from there?"

"I can land!"

"No, you can't. I have seen the way you 'land' and it is not a pretty sight."

"Why don't you go pick on Und? He's almost a quarter of the way up!"

"Und may not be able to climb as high as you yet but he knows how to land."

Trinon pouted and tried wiggling his way out of Mota's arms. He was flicked hard in the forehead, making him yelp and bring tears to his eyes. Und stopped climbing to look their way, a dead expression on his face. He hung securely from the wall almost lazily. This apparently made Trinon jealous and angrier. He had yet to master digging his claws in deep enough to hold on like that even though he could get up quite high faster.

His thoughts were so transparent that Mota flicked him again and carried his crying bundle to the washing chamber for the little ones. Trinon was filthy, covered in gravel and sweat. He also stunk which kept Mota from bringing him forward for Jaron to see. Their mother had a sensitive nose these days. Once they entered the washing room, Mota fought trying to undress him.

The wailing between flicks and rough housing brought their mother into the chamber looking annoyed at the noise. She bent down and came nose to nose with Trinon.

"Stop it!" she hissed. Her direct stare made him stop in mid tantrum. She turned to Mota. "You better make sure he is clean, understood?" Mota also went speechless, so nodded his head. Jaron left the room.

"That was scary, huh?"

Trinon gulped and nodded. There was no more fighting while Mota washed him up except when it came to cleaning behind the ears. There was some protest.

Und came in and observed the scene from the doorway. It amused him to see the dynamic between his two brothers. He was more like their father, quiet yet fierce and that's why Mota didn't spot him on the wall much. If anyone came to check on his progress it was Jakar.

Und could see why everyone focused on Trinon. If he could master his climb and landing, he would be just as great a warrior as their father. His temper needed some work though. For such a small manbeast, Und prided himself on being more intelligent than his siblings. He sat on the dirt floor at the entrance and waited for the two of them to finish so he could take his bath alone.

Without knocking or announcing his entrance, Modas entered Chardon's chamber to find their leader soaking in the large circular basin built into the floor. It protruded up at least two feet making it four feet deep. A ledge ran the perimeter on the inside of it.

Chardon was in female form with her head thrown back and eyes closed. Her skin had an almost golden sheen to it blending with the incoming sunlight. He noticed because she was flushed with ecstasy. It made his skin crawl knowing who she thought of at that moment. He spoke, jolting her out of her reverie.

"The council wants a meeting."

Water swished out of the basin onto the floor as Chardon abruptly sat up in surprise. Her eyes burned with anger when she turned her head to acknowledge his presence. Modas stood motionless. She eased forward out of the water, exposing her full nakedness, then leaned over to grab her covering robe on the opposite wall. Chardon never bothered to dry off and most days wringing water out of her hair was good enough.

"I really don't appreciate you coming in unannounced."

"My apologies."

"It's disrespectful and obviously intentional."

"That is not my…"

"Did you not all have a good laugh at my expense?"

Chardon turned around to face him from across the basin. He was back in male form.

Modas narrowed his eyes. "I did not find it amusing."

"Your family did."

He came around to the changing curtain and dressed in his council robes on top of the covering robe. He apparently had no inclination to stay with the council any longer than necessary and return to his chamber after the meeting.

"Let's go." He didn't wait for Modas to answer him.

"You trimmed your hair." Modas noticed it as Chardon came towards him to leave.

"Yes, well it would have been a nuisance during battle." With that he left the chamber.

Modas glanced at the basin made by Chardon's request, suggested by Halfar long ago. This was the first time Modas had seen it, let alone being used.

Walking after Chardon he could tell his leader was struggling with demons of his own. Secrets were something that could tear a planet apart and he knew why he had to keep this one.

Chardon's mate was not who she had seemed. Modas wanted to kill her many times over, her reach was long in the galaxy, she made sure of that. It was all in the guise of being a loving mate to Chardon who she despised for his diplomacy.

Falling in love with Halfar was probably inevitable.

Their race could not know just how horrid their beloved Sestis was and their leader being a shifter in love with the enemy who nearly destroyed them. They reached the council room and Modas took his place by the doorway to stand guard. He remembered when he had first learned of Halfar and Chardon's secret rendezvous.

It was a late afternoon with everyone involved in the negotiations taking a much-needed rest. Modas had just finished escorting Halfar and his entourage back to the gate. The council wanted to have another session to discuss the proposals Halfar suggested and he could not find Chardon.

On a whim, he had gone to Chardon's personal chamber to see if he was in there. And Chardon was there; in female form. The fact that she was naked didn't bother him; it was the smell coming off her, permeating the room. She seemed to have passed out in the process of trying to clean herself off. Candles flickered even though it was not yet sunset.

"What have you done?"

Modas covered his nose with the sleeve of his robe. He fought the urge to gag, feeling his throat contract from nausea.

Chardon turned her glazed eyes towards him, her body still flushed with sweat from mating. She tried to sit up, her body not listening. One arm flung out from the under the bed covering to dangle on the side of the bed. Modas braved the stench to get closer to her so he could hear her speak. Her lips were moving.

"You can't…" Was what he heard.

"Something is wrong with you."

He turned to leave in search of help and Chardon's iron grip held him by the wrist.

"You can't."

Her eyes pleaded with him even as he saw them go off far away and her body arched slightly on the bed. A breath sounding like a moan escaped her lips and she thrashed about for a split second from an orgasm. Mota wanted to wrench away from her, her actions tossing up more of the vile smell.

"You reek of something unnatural. You need to clean yourself off, now!"

"I'm trying."

"The council is reconvening by sunset to discuss Halfar's proposal," Modas hissed at her.

"Help me up." He yanked her out of bed and into the washing station next to the changing curtain. "I'm sorry." She whispered. "Thank you." Her eyes glanced back at him. "I'm still beautiful, am I not, Modas?"

A mischievous smile crept on her lips.

"I'll wait outside." He stopped. "We have to eliminate that stench."

He knew she was not listening since now her focus was on getting clean and shifting back into her male form, his failure to answer her question forgotten. From the window he saw the field of herbs nearby and dashed out to grab a hand full.

Back in Chardon's chamber, he burned the herbs and waved them throughout every corner of the room. A small amount he didn't burn went into the wash basin Chardon was using. There was a bowl of powdered ice near the bed, so he picked it up and dumped some of it on her. Chardon stood erect from the shock and back handed Modas with such unexpected strength that he flew backwards into the wall on the opposite side of the room. The bowl and remaining ice landed on each side of him.

Chardon's body shook from the chill and rage. It immediately vanished as she came to her senses. He could see the clarity return to her eyes. She finished cleaning herself off and dressed in council robes at the same time reverting into male form. It was a seamless transformation.

"You will tell no one!" He said it soft enough for Modas to hear with an edge of anger.

"Understood." Modas wiped a trickle of blood from the corner of his mouth.

"After you," Chardon motioned towards the doorway. His body trembled slightly.

Modas closed the door after them and helped Chardon whenever he faltered. It would have been better if he could rest until the end of the day. The council waited.

Pale skin ran the lines of the now closed wounds where new skin had begun to form. Talas studied every section and decided it wasn't so bad. The patterns left from the scars made them look like imprints in his skin. His admiration was witnessed by Kelin standing near the changing curtain.

"Does it make you proud to have survived the wrath of the manbeast?"

"He is right, it is a reminder though not the way he wanted. It gives me resolve." Talas twisted his naked body to get a better view in the harshly made mirror. The surface was not as clear as the ones on Earth. They made due with the resources their new planet had to offer. "Not to your liking, my beloved?"

Kelin walked over and traced the white scars with his index finger. He went around from back to front until they were face to face.

"Nothing can ever take away your beauty." He replied softly.

"How wonderful to hear." Talas encircled him in his arms and they touched foreheads.

"By the way, I was right."

"About what?"

"My theory, about Chardon."

Talas leaned back. "How do you figure?"

"He basically avoided answering my question. He is just as guilty as we are."

"You asked him outright?"

"It was a window of opportunity."

"Hmmm. I think you should have waited a bit longer."

"What secret could be so dire that even Modas has to keep it?"

Talas pulled away from him and dressing in a covering robe sat on the bed.

"Did it not seem odd to you that Chardon has not mourned the death of his beloved mate? It's as if he couldn't care less."

Kelin's eyes opened wider than normal. The idea of someone not mourning their mate seemed extreme. No matter how much you may disagree, that person was still your mate and Sestis was beloved by their people. Her core and vessel had been destroyed yet at the memorial ceremony, her name was never mentioned by Chardon or anyone else from the council.

"I think you need to figure out what is really going on. You'd think we would have had a separate mourning for Sestis by now. We didn't, and no one has brought it up yet so we all just continue forgetting about her."

He saw Kelin's temple wrinkle deep in thought.

"Was it something that Chardon did or was it something Sestis did?" Kelin paced.

"Maybe both." Talas shrugged.

"She was harmless. Her soft nature could do no wrong."

"Just so you know, she was not all that soft."

Kelin whipped around in shock.

"What do you mean?"

"I saw her grab a little one and shake him until he went limp, all for running into her while playing with some friends. They were chasing each other, and he was on the tail end. I guess no one except me saw it happen."

"That's…" Kelin advanced on him with such speed, Talas fell backwards on the bed. Kelin was on top of him eyes boring into him. "Why would you not say anything to anyone?" He yelled.

"No one would ever believe me. I was not well liked to begin with, remember?"

"So, our beloved Sestis was some sort of monster? What does that have to do with Chardon's guilt over our world being destroyed because of our stupidity?"

"If Halfar saw my displeasure in Chardon's decision making, don't you think he would have gone to Sestis as well? She felt Chardon was being too steadfast with the negotiations. He was not going to budge."

"We were just pawns in a big scheme?"

Kelin frowned then a new expression replaced it.

Talas almost laughed at how adorable Kelin looked all confused and awe struck when he asked it.

"Afraid so, my beloved." Talas sat up, his lips so close to Kelin's. "You must not confront anyone with this. If they think you know more than they think you do, it could get messy. I need you to stay safe."

He kissed him softly, teasingly until Kelin settled down on top of him. They both knew there was no point in arguing at this junction since mating was far more important.

Impatience

He could feel it, the agitation of knowing Chardon was coming for him soon. Halfar paced his bed chamber slowly, making sure to plant one foot in front of the other with every step. This had to be done since the last time he paced around thinking of Chardon he nearly injured himself by running into the edge of the bed and he was far from clumsy. Chewing on his lower lip became an annoying habit he could not seem to break over the past few years, never letting anyone else see him do it.

There was movement outside his chamber in the hall forcing him to instantly cease his inner deliberations. He stood at the doors and waited for what he assumed was a troop of Kur's enforcers escorting their commander to him, and he was right. The doors flung open and Kur nearly knocked Halfar down, except he came face to face with him and halted, a look of despair washing over his face. It was obviously meant to be an ambush.

As they both stood in that moment eye to eye, Halfar tilted his head to one side, not disengaging the stare. He saw the enforcers in the hall ready to strike and from Kur's back, his talons protruded out. Kur had a look of disbelief as he looked down at his chest and saw Halfar had indeed run him through.

"You seem to have come unannounced, yet again, despite my orders to not do so ever again."

"My lord," Kur managed to get out.

"Now, I am willing to forget this matter if you are ready to obey me." Kur was having trouble breathing as he replied, "Of course, my lord."

The enforcers were confused.

Halfar withdrew his claw and Kur collapsed in a heap unconscious in the doorway.

"Take him away." He barked at the enforcers.

Four of them hurriedly grabbed their commander and dragged him down the hall as they headed towards the healers. A thick trail of dark purple blood streaked the white floors. The rest turned in unison and marched back down the hall from whence they came.

"Rass!" Halfar summoned in his booming voice.

"My lord?" Rass was at the end of the hall watching the retreat and carrying of Kur. "That was entertaining." He came forth.

"Make sure he is well guarded and well maintained."

"You wish to keep him on as a General?"

"For now, yes." Glancing at him, "Why did you not stop him?"

"I was certain you would handle the situation quickly."

"Why would he do something so detrimental to his wellbeing?"

Rass stepped past Halfar and sat on the edge of his bed. "When you shut down the barrier, Kur was in position to take control of a nearby city in one of his regions. The barrier revealed them almost instantly, so he probably assumed you had done it on purpose to dispatch him."

"Paranoia."

"Understandable when you are trying to overthrow your ruler without anyone suspecting."

"That was how long ago?"

"Kur does like to hold a grudge."

"I thought that was against his aesthetics?"

"Hardly." Rass removed himself from the bed and headed down the hallway. "I will go attend to him and make sure he lives."

"Do not antagonize him." Rass made a face. "I mean it, Rass."

A wave of his general's hand was his reply.

Kelin was not one to sit around and wait for the inevitable so he went straight into Chardon's battle room and demanded an answer. He didn't care if it was premature, a battle was nearing, and he needed to know what exactly he was fighting for.

"Tell me, Chardon, what kind of tragedy did Sestis bring upon us? I now know for a fact that she was not the sweet natured regent everyone thinks!" Chardon's shocked expression was enough for him to continue. "Don't you think we deserve to know?"

Chardon cut him off right there. "To know what? That she was a monster? That our world became a target because of her actions? Are you going to tell our people, who loved her more than they loved or trusted me, their leader?"

Slacked jawed, Kelin moved away from the table he had slammed his fists on to get Chardon's attention. It never occurred to him the ramifications of that information and Talas had warned him time was a sensitive matter. The people may not believe anything he or Chardon said. The other side of the coin was they would hate her. Hate was a strong emotion needing no fuel since their world was destroyed and what was left of their race now resided on a planet with a weak sun.

"But, I…" Kelin was now lost for words.

"It has come up to grant her a memorial. I tried to

avoid it by averting everyone from her memory. With a new harvest the workers wanted an offering since she loved the field workers."

"No she didn't!" Kelin spat out, remembering the story Talas told him.

"Doesn't change the fact they think so."

"How did her actions end up having our world targeted? And for what?"

Taking a seat closer to Kelin he explained.

"When we went on diplomatic visits to other worlds, Sestis would use her charm to manipulate, blackmail and connive her way into getting whatever she wanted. Sometimes it was to get resources that should have gone to a needy planet rerouted to ours, so we would have a monopoly on certain ones. She did all of this in my name and our race, boasting of our unique powers. Over time, animosity brewed and when they threatened our world she did not back down. In fact, she welcomed their wrath."

"That's insane! Wait," Kelin shook his head. "How does Halfar come into this?"

"Halfar saw what she was doing and didn't like it. If our world was going to be conquered, better he do it to ensure our race than a hostile one hell bent on vengeance to wipe us out."

"He was the one who ended up nearly wiping our race out of existence."

"Negotiations did not go well."

"Because of Sestis?"

Incredible, Kelin thought to himself.

"Yes," Chardon sighed heavily.

Kelin saw that was all he was going to tell him. There was no reason to say any more. He was suddenly exhausted. Kelin saw it on Chardon's face as well.

"I'm sorry you feel this way, Chardon. Regardless, the people have to know eventually."

He walked out of the battle room in turmoil over what he had discovered. It never came across as this bad when he ran the scenarios of what the secret could be. Knowing this, he hoped Chardon could postpone the memorial for as long as he could.

Back with Talas in their chamber, he relayed everything that was told to him and watched Talas start to pace. At first, he was angry at his mate for pushing the subject, then listened more intently.

"Such insanity!" Talas was flabbergasted among other things. "Who else knows this, again?"

"Chardon, Modas and now us."

"You mean, Jaron and Ganna have no clue?"

"I'm not sure but I think they are the last two who need to know."

"No, our people are the last who need to know because it would be chaos."

"The workers want a memorial offering ceremony for Sestis."

Talas' eyes became saucers.

"Over my scorched corpse!"

"Chardon is trying to postpone it for as long as he can. They will not accept rejection without an explanation."

"Then he has to do that."

"What?"

"Explain!"

"Talas, there has never been a rebellion in the history of our race. This could damage us all."

"It doesn't matter. Either way, our race has to face the truth and reestablish ourselves without a false benevolent regent to hold on to."

Modas leaned against the wall of Chardon's chamber."

"You told him?"

"Not everything. I told him about Sestis' interplanetary frolics."

"A memorial would be a disaster."

"We will have one and tell them much of the truth before the offerings."

"That's madness."

"Your warriors will be there to handle any outbreaks."

"I will not harm my own people."

Chardon sighed. It was getting harder to talk to anyone let alone command them.

"Please. It will be sorrowful enough as it is."

The time to implement their battle plans finally arrived and Ganna was all over the place making sure everything was set to simultaneously open five vortices. She would open the one for the main gate while the others were going to be created by revived workers a bit rusty on the uptake. They had been practicing on a smaller scale for nearly three years and not all the kinks were ironed out. It would have to do for now. As long as their warriors ended up in the correct sectors, it should be okay.

Talas was in full battle gear wearing a tan brown sleeveless robe over a skin-tight tunic. There were two long swords crisscrossed on his back held by leather straps. His dirty blond hair was still damp and hung stringy across his shoulders, down his back. Kelin was in similar gear except his attire was all black minus weapons because he was an energy user. They stared at each other in silence as their assignments required them to be apart for the duration of the battle.

Modas kept an audience of twenty warriors as he relayed their tasks. Mota and Jakar listened diligently while sharpening their claws on pieces of stone. Those were the only deadly items a manbeast needed. On the other side of the field, Jaron and Mara led a group of energy users in a last-minute practice run. Everyone seemed ready.

Chardon was alone in the council room head in his hands as he sat on a bench near the window. His body was shaking, and he didn't know why. He was confused yet resolved at the same time. Tears stung his eyes and he fought them back. With everything that had happened over the course of a year, he should not be surprised.

It took a lot of coaxing to stop people from desecrating Sestis' memorial when the truth became known, Chardon glad the rest of what she had done remained secret. He took a sharp intake of air that forced him to look up and he saw the muted sunlight trying to illuminate the room. He stared at it for a long time.

"Multiple vortex openings have been identified." Rass reported.

The throne room was eerily quiet without Kur's enforcers running around and Halfar liked it that way. It gave him time to think. He glanced over at Rass, still bowed low on one knee.

"How many?"

"They have not been pinpointed yet."

Halfar tapped his index finger to his lips.

"Focus on any signature close to the palace."

"Then what?"

"Nothing. It would be the one Chardon appears from."

"With a troop of warriors, one possibly being that manbeast."

"No, when you intercept the signatures, you are going to do a bit of rearranging."

"You mean, as soon as all parties are outside of the vortex, we transport them. Random?"

"No." Halfar half turned to him. "Make sure the four of them are back together, without Modas."

"Ahh." Rass had an inkling of what Halfar had in mind. "They should be given an explanation after all that has transpired."

"I only need ten enforcers and you in the throne room to ensure no one does anything," he paused for the right word, "foolish."

"What about the other vortex signatures?"

"I'm sure the enforcers, along with Kur, will keep them busy."

As Rass left to do his bidding, he thought of how Kur would fare with the manbeast. He had no doubt of Kur's capabilities but a manbeast was something else entirely. Kur might actually enjoy the battle and forget about the incident where he tried to kill his ruler.

The vortex on the east side of the palace ripped open to produce Talas and his army. They were ten strong and ready for a fight. Talas set foot in front of the east wall and was attacked with his men not getting any better treatment. He drew one of his long swords and headed straight into the middle to gain leverage. After taking out three enforcers, a burst of light engulfed him, and he vanished. His army, surprised, was caught off guard and vulnerable as enforcers clambered down the walls towards them.

On the north Kelin suffered the same fate while going head to head with some of Halfar's more formidable human servants. A few enforcers were mixed in and he was able to take down two of them before being taken and replaced by

Mota. Their well-structured plans turned into chaos.

Kur sent his enforcers to intercept the intruders from all sides. All along the palaces' perimeter a battle ensued causing destruction to its walls and the area surrounding it. Kur made his way down to the West side and had to bend backwards to avoid a wide angled swipe of talons. Stepping back, he caught a glimpse of Jakar before the manbeast came at him relentlessly. Kur was pleased to finally let off some steam and fight the way he wanted. He was having fun.

At the main entrance to Halfar's palace, the vortex opened with Chardon, Jaron and Modas along with seven warriors that included Mara. In an instant, they were ambushed by Rass and his enforcers. Modas took a group of four on his side while Mara used her energy to create a shield for Chardon. Midair about to strike a fatal blow to an enforcer, the manbeast and Mara were swept up, vanishing in thin air to be replaced by Talas and Kelin. Once again, all four were together under the Earth sky.

"What's going on?" Kelin hollered in fear.

He was still in an attack stance, enforcer blood spotting his robes.

This was not supposed to happen.

Modas was transported to Talas' regiment right in the middle of an attack. He had no time to regroup so used his might to drive the enforcers back. In the recesses of his mind he cursed whoever did this to leave Chardon vulnerable. He was sworn to protect his leader with his life if necessary despite their differences. Slicing an enforcer in half, black blood splattering over him, he advanced into the horde to find a way out and back to the main doors.

Mota fared no different as he appeared where Kelin had been only to find himself surrounded by a large number of enforcers and human servants. Some had sharp thin long swords which made them part of the Asian crime syndicates Talas and Kelin had referenced. He extended his claws and dropped down into attack position. These men did not look like the type who scared easily.

Chardon turned abruptly to all sides looking for the culprit, finding no one. Seeing who was now in his party, it made sense. This was Halfar's will. All the enforcers present backed off, which meant he wanted them to get inside without incident. He motioned to Kelin and Talas.

"Lead the way. You know where the throne room is, correct?"

Regaining their composure, both men assumed defense stances, Kelin covering the front, Talas the rear. No way were they taking any chances on Halfar just letting them waltz in. All around them there was silence and it disturbed Chardon. As they moved into the palace itself, soft sounds of awe echoed through the halls of the magnificent building. At the entrance to the hallway leading to the throne room everyone stopped.

Rass stood blocking their path with ten enforcers. His smile was somewhat wicked as he bowed and moved to the side motioning them in. The enforcers closed rank after Chardon, Jaron, Talas and Kelin passed Rass. Footsteps clacked against white marble floors making the silence more prominent. The throne room doors were flung open to reveal Halfar lazily sprawled on the throne, his battle gear gone. Even Rass raised an eyebrow at that.

"You're probably wondering how this has happened." He swung his legs forward and sat with his legs spread wide apart. "You see, I didn't want that manbeast to come in here and tear things up." He leaned further towards them. "And I think I should explain. I wanted the four of you here to understand how you ended up on this planet without your cores."

"This was your doing?" Jaron seethed. "How?"

"I wanted to extract you before the bomb hit and did not know how. Rass came up with a way in short time. I didn't know it would grab just your body and leave the core."

"Why would you extract us?"

"He didn't do it on purpose." Kelin replied.

"He only wanted Chardon." Talas completed the thought.

"That is correct. I am glad more of you were captured in the transport. I can't imagine the devastation Chardon would endure if your race had become extinct."

Jaron was confused.

"Why? Why just Chardon?"

Halfar caught Chardon's gaze and understood the whole truth had not been told. He wasn't sure if it was a benefit or hindrance. That look in Chardon's eyes said 'don't'.

"Let's finish our negotiations, shall we?"

Halfar stepped down and the sound of weapons being drawn filled the room. He looked around and Chardon saw his warriors ready to defend against the enforcers who reacted to the hostile act. Rass extended a transformed limb protruding deadly spikes and held it at Jaron, Talas and Kelin's throats.

"Now, now. We should be more cooperative. I'm sure my lord means yours no harm."

"So true." Halfar extended his hand to Chardon. "Come."

Chardon slowly walked to him, looking back once at his entourage held hostage by Rass and the enforcers. For the first time he felt a slight twinge of fear for his friends.

"No need to worry. No one is leaving this room until the two of you return." Rass promised.

The double doors to the hallway leading to Halfar's chamber were opened by two enforcers and they entered, the doors booming shut behind them. As they walked, they talked.

"Why are you doing this?" Chardon hissed softly.

Halfar leaned towards him and whispered into his ear. "I wanted to see you."

"What exactly are we negotiating? You destroyed our world." Halfar opened his chamber room and secured the doors once they were inside.

"I never wanted that to happen. I regret it more than you know." Chardon turned his back to him. "When I realized what I had set in motion, all I could think of was saving you over anyone else." Chardon swung around and backhanded him. The force tilted his head sideways. "I deserve more than that." Chardon made sure his eyes conveyed his fury and Halfar understood. "I played right into her hands. She still didn't win."

"No one won anything!"

Waiting no longer, Halfar grabbed Chardon's face and kissed him fervently, forcing Chardon to eventually submit. Chardon's body went limp as he shifted into female form. Halfar held her up with his arms kissing her neck, her breasts, all while she tried to feebly push him away. He hoisted her higher, tossing her onto the bed and yanked her robes off in one move. The tunic underneath he ripped to shreds with a lone talon he had extended. Sitting above her he removed his over shirt and leggings.

"You can't." Chardon pleaded softly.

Wrapping his hand around one of her ankles he dragged her towards him raising her leg to his shoulder. His gaze never leaving hers, his tongue spilled out and hung down nearly to the bed. She watched as its pointed end flicked between her thighs then entered her.

Gasping, her fingers took hold of the bed cover balling them in her fists. His tongue left her center and traveled up her body as he leaned forward to hover over her then back into his mouth. Their eyes stayed locked.

"No more visions," he seethed as a talon slid deep into her.

Her fists tighten again on the bed cover, her back arched and eyes squeezed shut.

"Look at me." He commanded. With difficulty, she took deep breaths and opened her eyes. "I missed you."

He withdrew the talon replacing it with what she really wanted: him. One hand flew from the bed and slammed into his chest, her nails digging into his flesh as he entered crudely. Her mouth gaped open in shock and he sealed it with his. She knew he was going to have every bit of her until he was satisfied.

The throne room maintained an eerie silence as all occupants dared not move. Rass had the entire perimeter surrounded with enforcers. One wrong movement would start an all-out battle Chardon's team knew they would not win.

"Why have they been gone so long?" Jaron was getting worried.

"Delicate negotiations should not be rushed." Rass explained.

"It has been over an hour!" Talas almost reached for his long sword again.

"Until they return, you will behave. Thirsty?" Rass turned to a human servant outside the main doors. "Bring some refreshments, please."

"Something is not right." Kelin kept looking around for clues.

"Whatever they wish to discuss is not of our concern."

Rass leaned against a wall, arms crossed.

"This is unacceptable!" Jaron collected threads of energy.

"You will wait!" Rass bellowed, silencing all. A cart arrived at that moment with drinks. "Now, let's have a nice chat together."

He was also puzzled by the long wait until he realized what might be occurring in his lord's bed chamber. It had been awhile since they were together. Knowing that, he sat down for the long haul. Halfar was not going to waste one moment, so Rass figured it would be at least another two hours before they emerged from that hallway. He grinned.

No one could hear Chardon's screams of pain and pleasure except Halfar. It fed his hunger for her and he touched every inch of her body with his own. They had never been able to experience mating of such magnitude because they had always needed to hold back in fear of being caught. With utter abandon, Chardon let Halfar do whatever he wanted to her, even acts of sexual depravity she never knew could be done. Their body fluids mingled, coating every inch of the bed.

Exhaustion took them instantly as they reached the final throws of orgasm together for the third time. Their bodies shuddered from overexertion. Side by side, they tried to breathe normally and not choke on their own spittle. Halfar laid his hand on her exposed thigh and caressed it. Chardon pushed it away not bothering to turn her head to see what he was thinking. Her chest hurt, it was on fire inside. She hiccupped and cried.

"Shh."

Halfar rolled onto his side to wipe drenched hair from her face. Not being able to help himself, his left hand clutched one of her breasts and softly squeezed though not enough to hurt. He kissed her shoulder blade while his hand moved slowly down to rest between her thighs. She cried out in surprise and gasped sharply for air. Her hand instinctively went to stop him going further.

"If I had the energy to devour you, I would."

"Let me go."

"I will, soon. First we need to calm you."

He reached into the cabinet on her side of the bed and produced a tiny vial.

"No," she breathed, "don't do this." She clasped his hand and the vial with hers.

"Are you going to reunite with your group like this? You will need this to shift back."

"No."

"Why"

"I can't." Chardon was scared. "My body won't…"

Halfar sat up and looked around the chamber. He had an idea. Taking the dropper out of the vial, he tipped it down to her mouth. She tried to turn away as he held her head steady until half of it was consumed. Her body immediately relax, her breathing slowed to normal. On the floor were the remnants of her tunic so he used them to wrap her breasts down tight until she appeared nearly flat chested. Luckily the fabric was unforgiving, albeit causing discomfort.

"It hurts."

"I know."

He helped her back into her robes noticing her eyes starting to glaze over. She was going to fall unconscious if he didn't get her back home soon. Redressing and making sure Chardon could stand, he opened the doors and led her back to the throne room. He had not planned on their negotiations to turn out this way. Once he had her alone, there was no turning back until he had fulfilled his ultimate agenda.

The double doors opened. Rass stood and bowed while Chardon's entourage retook their defensive positions with weapons drawn and energy spheres formed ready to strike. Seeing this, Rass motioned with just his head and his small army encircled them. Glancing over he could tell Chardon was not well.

"What have you done to him?" Jaron demanded raising one hand with a spinning ball of energy.

Halfar smirked. "Your leader is just fine."

Chardon moved away from him to his group. "We must leave."

"Chardon!" Kelin made ready to strike.

"Now!" Chardon continued moving forward, his group surrounding him as he went, keeping an eye on Rass and his enforcers who also watched them retreat. "There's no time to regroup."

Outside of the palace Jaron created a vortex as fast as she could and closed the opening right as the last man stepped into it. She would send a signal for Ganna to open vortexes to retrieve the others.

Gears of Change

Back on New Lassa, Jaron tried to get Chardon to speak to her. She could tell something was not right. Her pleas to go to the medical chamber were ignored. Talas and Kelin were no help. Both kept giving each other strange looks and watched Chardon go directly to the housing commons.

Chardon barely made it to her chamber and didn't have the mind to secure the main door before getting into bed. Under the covers, she removed her robes and the constricting fabric, tossing them on the floor. The vibrations that started coursing through her body earlier intensified. She fought hard to stop it before falling into deep sleep, not hearing anything that transgressed outside before the darkness of night as the council scrambled to get their battle squads back. No one disturbed her.

"Did you get it?"

Halfar sat upright on his throne as Rass entered. He was tense again. A few hours with Chardon was not nearly enough to satisfy him. Finding the planet was of great importance now.

"Of course." Rass bowed. "I will relay the coordinates to you."

"Good." Halfar relaxed a bit. "Thank you for holding them at bay."

"I was certain you did not want to be intruded upon."

Rass leaned closer and whispered. "So?"

"It's done."

"Ahead of schedule don't you think?"

"It couldn't be helped."

"Hmm? I didn't know you lacked such restraint." Rass stood. "Now what?"

"We wait. I will not have her life jeopardized."

"By the way, Kur is not happy that the festivities were so short lived."

"This is just the beginning. Earth is about to become a battle field."

"We are only taking over this region, correct?"

Halfar's eyes turned into slits of hate.

"It seems, Kur has made a plea to the council and MY advisors on our home world are sending MY armada to enslave Earth. We have not conquered a world in some time and this, apparently, is a better time than any."

Rass' expression showed disagreement. He did not want to be assigned as warden to this awful rock. Halfar confirmed what had to be done just by looking at him.

"Don't worry, Kur can have it." Halfar tilted his head. "If, we capture this planet."

"Are you thinking sabotage?"

"I will not stand for my armada to be used without my consent."

"Your will is mine."

Rass beamed at the thought of deceiving Kur one last time.

The hallway was dark and quiet, made more so by the stealth of Modas moving down it towards Chardon's chamber. He entered smoothly and immediately noticed the stench of mating with something foul. Sitting on the side of the bed listening to the ragged breathing, Modas knew what kind of sleep she was in and would not awaken for at least a few days.

Keeping this secret was no longer an option. The medical workers, along with Ganna, would have to be informed. He stroked her sweat matted hair as if she were a little one and sighed with regret. This too should not have happened on his watch.

So many people were crammed in Chardon's chamber that Ganna demanded only those needed stay and the rest leave immediately. She did not want Chardon's sleep to be disturbed. That would be harmful to her and the unborn child. At the end of the ruckus, Jaron, Modas, their elder children, Talas, Kelin and Ganna remained in the chamber. Still too many for her taste.

"What's wrong with Chardon?" Jaron chewed her lower lip as she stared at the bed. She showed signs of deep worry.

"Well, how shall I put this?" Ganna paused.

"Halfar did something to him. He didn't look right when he came back." Kelin interjected.

Talas had crept over to the side of the bed to get a closer look and was leaning over Chardon. Ganna yanked him back away from the bed.

"She's incubating! You cannot touch her!"

There was silence, then sharp intakes of air. Talas turned to Modas knowing what the secret was he held. Jaron, still speechless, sat down on a pillow chair near the window.

Kelin had an epiphany about the so-called negotiations before their world was destroyed.

"Halfar is in love with Chardon." He blurted out for all to hear.

"More importantly," Talas raised a finger and pointed at the bed, "Chardon is a shifter."

"A shifter!" Jaron finally cried out. "Chardon is a shifter?" Finally catching on to what Ganna meant by incubating. Her head snapped around towards Modas.

"But, Sestis…" Jaron began.

"Knew." Was all Modas had to say.

Jaron's face had turned a few shades of dark pink. It was clear how furious she was to know her mate had kept this from her, let alone Chardon.

"She seems to be in pain."

Talas had moved closer again.

"She's exhausted. Now, all of you, out! Jaron, help me get her into a more comfortable position."

The men left so the two women could tend to their leader. Jaron tried to lift Chardon's legs to turn them and was shocked at how heavy they were. She met Ganna's gaze.

"She's like dead weight. Ganna, is she really okay?"

"I can't know for sure until she wakes up. Until then we have to keep a constant watch."

They were able to get her on her back with her head propped up on pillows. Jaron found her covering robe to dress her in and got it on with Ganna's assistance.

Outside, Kelin sat with his head in his hands shaking it back and forth while Talas walked around in a circle next to him. So many thoughts were going through both their minds as they processed all that had happened.

"My theory was right." Kelin spoke first.

"Of course it was, beloved. I know you could have never guessed this."

"Not in all of eternity." He looked up from his reverie. "What does this mean?"

"That there are more secrets."

"What else could there possibly be?"

"Think, beloved. Sestis, Modas and Halfar knew that Chardon was a shifter. They also knew what kind of a monster Sestis was. The next part is easy."

A light bulb lit up in Kelin's head.

"Sestis had something to do with the negotiations going south and Halfar deciding to destroy us all."

"Bingo!" It was an Earth term he had picked up and thought appropriate for the occasion.

"Yes, but what was it and how? How could we have been so blind as to not see her for what she was?"

"That and more," Talas replied. "You know what I think?" Talas bent down to him and their eyes met. "You look exhausted. You should go to bed."

"Ahh, and will you be joining me?"

"Why, of course my beloved. Come, too much thinking is going on and not enough mating."

"I think Chardon and Halfar did enough of that for all of us." Kelin muttered.

Talas wagged his finger as he led Kelin back to their chamber.

"No, no. We must all do our own fair share in our own way. Yes?"

Kelin stopped talking the rest of the way.

"I want to fight too!"

Trinon had both arms straight down on his sides, his little head tilted as far back as it could go in order to stare up into Mota's face.

Mota laughed loudly, throwing his head back.

"Of course you do!" He leaned forward until he was at a ninety-degree angle, his nose nearly touching Trinon's. "You are not ready." Trinon lunged at him, and an arm appeared grabbing him up so that he dangled sideways.

"Until you can land properly and climb, it is as he says," their father bellowed.

Modas brought his son's body up until they were eye to eye. Trinon relented without struggle and his father put him down.

"This battle will not rage long, and you shall never see it. There will be more, and you must be ready."

He glanced back at Mota as he walked away. They nodded to each other.

"Up you go," Mota said and without warning, grabbed Trinon and tossed him into the air towards the wall.

He may not be as small as he used to be but Mota was twice his size. Trinon hit the wall hard and, as he scrambled to grasp hold, caught sight of Und with his back against the wall holding on with the claws of his fingers and toes.

Mota shook his head seeing the jealousy in Trinon's expression.

"Focus on yourself, little one."

"I am not little!"

He caught a piece of wall and secured himself on it, his face red with anger.

☼

The Americas, parts of Asia and Europe were in turmoil as enforcers took over territories with little effort. The human's military might was nothing compared to Halfar's. Government science divisions had detected the giant mother ship outside of Earth's orbit and speculations flew. Only a select few in his fold knew what it was and who it belonged to.

Halfar's armada had arrived much to his disgust. It had been three months since Chardon had been on Earth and Halfar made sure the gate was blocked so no one from her planet could come through. He could open the gate from his end when he needed to check up on her. Kur was becoming unmanageable again and he had to decide soon. He couldn't let his general know about his plans just yet.

Ganna ran to the gate console filled with fear as the guards and she watched the vortex open, dark figures marching forward through the gate. It reminded her of when their planet had been destroyed before they knew what had really happened. She was confident in knowing who the first figure would be and she was right.

Halfar emerged from the gate with an entourage of eight bodyguards following him. The smugness in his appearance made Ganna twitch with disgust. In human form he still managed to get that result from off-worlders. He smiled at her as a greeting and bypassed her, moving onward to the housing commons.

"I don't need an escort to Chardon's chamber," he stated. "I can smell her even from this distance."

Workers who remembered him stared in confusion and fear as he strode into the building. In the hallway, Modas was guarding the doorway. Ganna smirked as he gauged the manbeast up close and saw the realization of just how formidable he was. The look on Modas' face suggested they would not be on friendly terms. Halfar stepped back from him a bit.

"I need to see her."

Modas sneered at him, opening the door and moving sideways to allow him access. From the doorway they could see the rise and fall of her ribcage as she breathed softly. Behind the sheer fabric surrounding her bed, she lay still in deep slumber with pain and exhaustion etched in her facial expression.

"What's wrong? Why is she still incubating?"

He directed his question to the medical worker. Upon further observation of the room, Chardon's usual group was found spread around the chamber. Instead Jaron answered.

"You tell us, you monster. This is your doing!"

"Impregnating her is one thing, I am speaking of why she is this way," he snapped.

Ganna came into the chamber and went directly to check Chardon's forehead.

"She had a fever for a few weeks and did wake up on one or two occasions. I think it is because her body has not yet fully regained itself as female. It is quite possible Chardon did not shift often to female form to keep it acclimated."

"No, she wouldn't. All for the sake of your race, and HER."

They all knew who he meant. He went around to the other side of the bed and sat next to Chardon's sleeping body. He brushed strands of hair from her face and stared down at her. Everyone in the room watched, feeling awkward, an audience to his show of affection for Chardon.

"I need to tell you something," Halfar began. "It is more like a proposal."

That got Ganna's and everyone else's attention. Even Modas came into the room from out of the hallway with a bang of the door swinging open. Last time Halfar made one it meant doom for their race. Another one was not a welcome invitation. He saw the looks on their faces and held up a hand.

"Shall I explain my dilemma?" They all froze. "My armada has been sent, without my approval, to Earth."

"How can it be without your approval?"

Kelin was not buying it any more than Ganna was.

"I have not yet explained." Halfar cast a glare at him. "May I continue?"

"My apologies," Kelin muttered noticing everyone staring at him, irritated.

"Conquering Earth was not my intention. One of my Generals, Kur, had found the planet and thought it was a great race to enslave. He initiated the conquest, so I came to investigate and assist."

"Thinking nothing of destroying yet another world." Ganna piped in to their dismay.

"For the love of Lassa!" Mara yelled, balling her hands into a fist.

Halfar continued. "That is true, I thought nothing of it. I also saw it as a way to flee from my advisors and the battles. I had your vessels which my other General, Rass, helped keep hidden from prying eyes. If anyone knew what I had done, extracting all of you, my reign as ruler would be put in question and I needed to stay in control. It is now clear that Kur has relayed this information to the royal advisors."

Jaron and Talas glanced at each other and Talas was the one to speak.

"You don't want to conquer Earth? Then why not tell them to withdraw?"

"Kur has engaged in a campaign to overthrow me and claim my armada for himself. He knows in his gut I would choose Rass over him."

"Preemptive strike." Talas deduced.

"Correct. I want to lose this battle, get rid of Kur and return my armada to its home base."

"So, what is your proposal?"

Halfar stood from his seat by the bed and turned to face them.

"I need you to attack my forces on all fronts before my armada deploys. Take out as many of Kur's enforcers as you can. Stopping his advance is key."

"You want us to murder your own kind, so you can run away?" Ganna spat.

"No." Halfar sighed in exasperation. "Kur's enforcers are replicated organisms unsanctioned by our people. I did not know about it until after the fact and by then, he had over a thousand created. Those abominations must be destroyed!" He took a deep breath and let it out slowly. "I want to stay here with Chardon and resume our interplanetary meetings. We have to try and correct the damage done by Sestis."

Ganna glanced over at Jaron who had a puzzled expression and not making any headway regarding the logistics of the whole battle plan. She saw Talas obviously thinking in the same context and he went over to tap Jaron. His expression told her he had a plan.

"There is one stark problem." Kelin interjected. "You sent a planet destroyer to our world and we have this," he spread his arms towards outside, "to try and live on. Have you seen the sun?"

"I never wanted that to happen. It was childish of me and it cost you greatly. I have no way of atoning for that. I can make this planet thrive for you, though."

"How?" Kelin opened his arms wide.

"When there is a way to destroy, there is a way to create. There is a 'bomb' for that as well."

"And what? You're going to use one of those for this planet?"

"In a way, yes."

"Uh-uh, I don't trust you." Kelin pointed a finger at him.

"You say you want to get off Earth and stay here. You do realize that would leave Earth in shambles? Your forces have not been kind," Talas continued where Kelin left off.

"If there is one thing I learned about humans is that they are resilient. Nothing keeps them down for long. They can rebuild." Halfar sat back down on the bed. "If it were not for Sestis…"

Modas' head snapped towards the others in the room and he made a quick decision. "I think you all should leave for a while." They turned to stare at him confused. "Chardon needs quiet."

"What about him?" An insulted Kelin barked.

"He is not disturbing her. We can discuss the rest of this matter later." He motioned for them all to exit and Ganna felt suspicious.

What are you up to manbeast? She asked in silence as she was the last to be forcibly pushed out the chamber.

Halfar raised his eyebrows at Modas when it was just the two of them and a sleeping Chardon.

"I have my reasons," Modas said.

"I was going to finish my explanation."

"I know."

"Do you not also want to know why I did it?"

"I already know."

"Then why?"

"They do not need to know any more about Sestis and her actions." Modas recalled the memorial that had turned into a disaster. The people were so distraught and angry it nearly became a mob. "She was like poison that no one knew was already in their veins."

"Keeping it from them won't change much."

"I disagree." Modas went to the door and as he closed it shut, "When you are ready to leave, I will be outside to escort you."

"I was not escorted in."

"No, but you should have been."

Modas closed the door and continued to stand guard in the hallway.

Chardon stirred when Halfar climbed into the bed with her, leaning over to stroke her hair. Her eyes fluttered open and there was a brief moment of recognition before he shook his head and coaxed her back to sleep. He laid a hand on the swell of her belly feeling the life inside move around.

Their two races had never procreated together, and he wondered, no worried, about the outcome. The thought of their offspring clawing its way out her, killing her in the process, made the color drain out of him. He had to come back and have a long talk with Ganna.

The sun was setting, and he knew it was time to go. Kissing Chardon on the forehead, he got up and went to meet Modas outside to be escorted back to the gate. He found it curious no one had asked how he opened the gate from the outside.

On a hill not far from the commune, Talas and Jaron sat on a boulder together. They felt odd being in such close proximity alone since the two were not friendly towards each other just yet. A sort of truce had been formed to get things done.

Talas walked a few inches from the boulder and poised himself on the edge of the hill, one leg bent at the knee from resting on a large stone near the edge. In reddish brown hide leather, his long sword hanging off one side, and his dirty blonde hair getting swirled around by the breeze he looked like the warrior he was. It did nothing for Jaron.

"Is it just me, or is your mate hiding more secrets for our leader?" He started.

"He is surely hiding something. The fact that he knew all of this makes me angry."

"What do you think about Halfar's proposal?"

"There is no way we can trust him!"

"Ahh," Talas used a finger to move away some fly away hair, "sure we can." He turned to her. "He loves Chardon more than anything in this universe and has for a long time. He kept all of us because if our world were dead, Chardon would at least have some of his race with him. I think, getting him off Earth would benefit us."

Jaron thought it over for a bit and nodded her head.

"The planning is the problem. How do we drive Kur off that rock without a scratch on our troops?"

"We will not come out of this one unscathed, my dear Jaron."

"I am not your dear!"

Talas let out a little laugh.

"So touchy. I have no interest in you, trust me." He saw the offended look on her face. "Not everyone finds you so beautiful. The same as Ganna detests me."

Returning to his gaze across the fields, he sighed and let the breeze wash over him. He crossed his arms and leaned forward, head tilted towards the sky.

"Stop that!" She snapped, and Talas peeked at her with one eye. "Why does everything you do have to be damn erotic?"

"I'm just standing here, dearie, on a hill." Jaron's eyes narrowed at him. "Fine." Talas went back to the boulder and sat down next to her. "Not unscathed. No casualties. I can guarantee that."

"Why is Kelin being so forceful these days?" Jaron changed the subject. It had been bothering her since they regained their cores how the lovers' dynamic had changed. "He always followed you."

"Not on Earth, he didn't." Talas cocked his head to one side. "I wonder. He's not a strategist like I am. On Earth, he seemed more knowledgeable." His forehead creased. "Of course, I was some sort of imbecile on that planet." It infuriated him just thinking about it. Jaron found it quite hilarious and started laughing heartily. "That's not very nice of you, dear."

"Sorry." Jaron wiped her eyes. "I just remember all of us wanting to smack you around for the sheer joy of it. We knew it would be wrong to bully you but, you made it so easy and I didn't feel the least bit guilty."

"How hateful."

"Without your core, you really were just an empty-headed shell of a being." Jaron slapped her knee and laughed again her head thrown back.

Restraining Chardon ended up being more of a hardship than Ganna, or the workers, had anticipated as they forgot how strong she was. Her hair had gotten long again and snagged on the bed covers every time Ganna was able to get her back down only to have her push back up more furious than before.

"Let go of me!"

"Chardon, you need to listen to me and calm down!"

"I need to find him!"

"You need to let me examine your unborn child and make sure it does not mean your demise as it enters this world."

Chardon stopped fighting for a moment staring at her in confusion.

"What do you mean?"

"Our two races have never mated before and if you haven't forgotten, Halfar's true form comes with claws."

"So do manbeasts!"

"Not like this!"

Chardon thought about it again and confirmed in her mind Ganna was correct. She could feel her unborn child moving around and the tiny claws, not yet sharp enough to rip open flesh, graze across the inside of womb. Breathing deep and letting it out slowly, she let her arms slip from Ganna's grip.

"I still need to see him."

"I am already here." Halfar stepped out of the shadows near the door with Modas in tow. "You really should stay in bed resting. Ganna and I have some details to go over."

"I…" Halfar leaned in and kissed her softly on the lips making her shiver. "You're coming back?"

"Of course." He turned to Ganna. "Let's proceed."

Ganna brought over the examination tablet and held it above Chardon's belly to get a good view of the fetus. Once the image was recorded along with vital signs for both mother and child, she left the room, with Halfar in tow, to the medical research chamber.

Halfar was silent the entire time and Ganna felt she may have misjudged the tyrant. It nagged her about why their planet had been destroyed on a whim and she had an awful suspicion that Sestis, yet again, was the cause.

She silently scrutinized the image in her research lab then made a suggestion.

"We can extract him when it is time."

"How?" Halfar tensed at the sound of it.

"Cut her open." The medical workers gasped in horror and Halfar rose from his seat. "Or," she reeled back; not liking what was about to occur, "we can carefully insert a membrane around the fetus to prevent him from clawing his way out of her."

"Will you sedate her?"

"Do you think she would let me?"

Ganna swirled around in her seat facing Halfar.

"No." He resumed his seat and tapped his lower lip. "I do have a way to ease her down."

An eyebrow shot up on Ganna's brow. "Please, explain."

"I had an elixir made that forces the biological system to slow down. Only a tiny bit is needed."

"You've used this elixir before then? On Chardon?"

"How did you think she was able to get back here without collapsing?"

"She did collapse! She barely made it to her chamber!"

"Don't be so dramatic! I knew the timeline and made sure there was enough in her to get her home. I am not a monster!"

"And that is what troubles me." It was Halfar's turn to seem confused. "Since you are not a monster, it makes me wonder why you sent that planet bomb."

"That was not my most glorious moment and I will regret it always." He hung his head defeated.

"Enough of that." Ganna waved her hand. "We have a new species to bring into our new world."

Und could see from his vantage point on the other end of the wall it was going to be bad. Trinon was angry and determined to prove everyone wrong by climbing the wall today when no one was watching. They didn't mind Und and his sister, Una, because they had a somewhat responsible nature. Trinon was another matter. The fighting had begun earlier that day.

"You are to stay put!" Mota had ordered Trinon as he left for a council meeting.

"Why can't I go practice with the others?"

"You want to know why?" Mota leaned down to face him. "You are not good enough or ready to climb on your own." He straightened. "That's why. Now go sit in the sandbox and play with the little ones or something."

Mota then strolled off, leaving a fuming Trinon to stand alone in the fields.

Und watched Trinon go to the sandbox while he went to the wall to practice. The look on his brother's face was nothing nice. So, it was no surprise that later in the day, Und saw him come up to the wall on the far end and stare up at it with mad fury. He attacked the wall with such speed even Und stopped climbing in a state of awe. It turned to dread as he saw how far up Trinon was.

A fall would be catastrophic.

The climb was going well and Trinon had a big grin on his face despite the sweat running down his back from the exertion. His claws clinked upward, and he was three quarters of the way up when one of his claws did not find a grip. He reached with the other hand and the claws also missed causing him to slide downward.

His body gained momentum. He was going to fall if he didn't do something fast. In a panic he tried desperately to find a grip as he continued down. Some of his claws on both hands snapped off as he went further down, the pain causing him to scream. Blood streaked down the wall and Und descended as fast as he could to try and reach him. It was no use. Trinon would have to land no matter how bad it would be. He turned his body and ended up sideways, his torn-up hands causing his form to be unbalanced.

Mota and Modas heard the screaming first and reacted before anyone else. As they neared the wall, Und was just touching down on the ground and headed towards Trinon still in free fall. He would not make it.

Mota took off at full speed with his father behind him and barely missed Trinon as he hit the bottom. By getting somewhat under him, he softened the fall. That was the least of their concerns. Trinon lay in his arms bloody and shaking from shock. The damage to his claws was alarming. Mota kept him close to his body to minimize the tremors and turned to their father.

The horror on Modas' face was nothing compared to the screams of Jaron as she rushed forward to them. All the blood everywhere is what caused her to scream, surely fearing her little one was dead. He stopped her midway and didn't let go as she fought to be released. Und stood wide eyed with grief.

"Get Ganna." Modas commanded Mota.

"I am here!" Ganna ran up out of breath. She too must have heard the screams. "Hurry, give him to me!" Mota did not move. He was also in shock. Ganna knelt to reason with him. "You have to give him to me! I need to treat him now!"

She laid a hand on his shoulder and felt the tension ease a bit. She motioned the medical workers who had followed her to hold him while she took Trinon out of his arms. They ran back to the medical chamber.

Jaron slid to the ground crying uncontrollably. Modas still held one of her hands in an iron grip without realizing it. His vision blurred, and he swayed. This had never happened before. Mota slowly stood up staring at his empty hands. Everyone was still until Modas let out a growl of such rage that the field workers nearby fled in fear of him going into a rampage. Und blinked for the first time since getting to the scene.

"I'm sorry." Mota whispered to Trinon. His hands trembled.

"It's not your fault, you know." Und said softly. "He just has a bad temper." Tears filled his eyes.

"Yes, it is."

Mota lifted his head to sky and saw the streaks of blood going down the face of the wall. A small cry caught in his throat and he couldn't stop tears from sliding down his face. Jakar came up behind him and rested his giant hands on his shoulders. After a moment, he went to pick Und up from where he stood frozen.

Pulling herself together, Jaron stood up and headed for the medical chamber. She stopped midway and turned to see if Modas was coming. A few seconds passed before he followed. They walked in silence as they made their way through the fields and down the slope that led to Ganna's operating room.

Inside, Ganna and the medics worked quickly to clean and close the wounds. Trinon lay on the table his eyes still open from the shock. Not a tear could be found. He had not cried through the whole ordeal his hands literally declawed. The look of defeat and resolve on Trinon's face told Modas what he already knew. Trinon would not give up, even now.

"He's doing so well, it kind of scares me." Ganna was finishing up with the bandages. On many wounds they were fine being closed. With manbeasts and their claws it was a lot more complicated. "I want to keep him sedated for a few days."

"Fine."

Modas touched Trinon's brow and traced their shape.

"Do not let him out of your sight! That boy is stubborn, and you know it."

"He won't be going anywhere."

Jaron kissed the top of his head. Modas left the room and she followed, neither saying a word. There would be no sleep tonight.

Jaron and Modas' children sat in the recreation room attached to their commune. The silence was deafening until a sniffle was heard. Una sat with her knees drawn in, head down on top. Und sat next to her, his legs stretched straight out, and arms laid flat on either side of him. Mara paced while chewing her nails. Jakar was trying to get Mota to snap out of whatever state he was now in. He would not speak, just sat on the floor staring into emptiness.

"I cannot understand what you are going through if you don't tell me." Mota's eyes rotated to Jakar's voice. "No one forced him up there. He needs to learn more discipline. This happens to be a horrible way for him to learn it."

"His claws may not grow back properly." Mara said between teeth and nail.

"He's stronger than he looks. Do not underestimate him. They will come back just as strong."

Mota finally moved by leaning forward and taking a shuddering breath.

"I pushed him too hard. It seemed like fun at the time …"

"He's hard headed and easily provoked. Reminds me of our departed brother."

"Yes, he is just like Hon," Mara piped up and laughed a little.

"Go see him." Jakar didn't yell yet Mota heard it as a command. He got up and left.

While going over scenarios on the tabletop holoscreen in the battle chamber, Rass heard footsteps echo through the hallway, leaving him little time to prepare himself for Kur's intrusion.

So, it's not just Halfar he ambushes, he thought to himself.

He turned his attention to the double doors and found Kur was already so close to him they shared the same breath. His eyes bore into Rass' like hot coals. Rass smiled at him sweetly.

"What may I…"

"Where is he?" Spittle flew into Rass' face and he calmly wiped it off. "You will tell me!"

"He is tending to some important business that does not pertain to you."

"I have searched this palace and this planet, and he is not here!"

"Surely, you are mistaken. Why don't you…"

"I will not be made a fool of!"

"Step away." Rass extended a razor-sharp talon at Kur's neck. This was tiring and irritating.

"Are you threatening me?"

Rass sighed and tilted his head to one side. Before Kur could react, he swung his arm and knocked him across the room into the wall.

"I told you to step away. Breathing the same air is not ideal for me." Using the same words Kur had said to him so long ago, he turned back to checking on Halfar's armada from his holoscreen. He heard the dragging of hard shell on marble floor. "Don't." He pulled out a plasma ray gun and aimed it at Kur without even looking at him.

The dragging stopped.

"You will regret this." He heard Kur seethe before the doors slammed shut and Rass was alone again.

When he felt Kur had gone far enough away from the battle room, Rass headed for the other side of the palace. In the hallway leading to Halfar's private chamber, Rass glanced at the indicator on his wrist telling him the secret gate he created was opening. He had to get there to close it right as Halfar stepped out before Kur could sense the vortex.

In conjunction with keeping a constant look out for movement around him he had to make sure none of Kur's enforcers, or the man himself, were following.

As he neared the hall, a gust of air blew in making a large sucking sound. Halfar stepped out of the vortex onto the palace floor and Rass typed in commands on his wrist band to close it. They stood face to face for a moment then Halfar turned.

"Walk with me," his ruler commanded.

"Kur has been scouring the planet and the palace for you. He even tried to attack me."

"Where is he now?"

"No idea." Halfar stopped short. "He did not follow me," Rass reassured him.

They continued their fast-paced walk to the throne room, bursting in to find Kur waiting for them. He smiled and bowed at Halfar.

"My lord, you were sorely missed today."

"I did not know I was expected to be in anyone's presence."

"You have been in the palace all this time?" He asked, his tone dripping honey.

Halfar's face twitched as he settled into his throne. "Where else would I be, Kur?"

"I am only concerned for your well-being in these tumultuous times. We are at war with the humans, as dull as that may be."

"There's an uprising off the coast of Spain. If you wish, I can dispatch my enforcers to regain the region." Rass interrupted. "I believe my army is better equipped to handle them."

Kur was not to be ignored.

"In that case, I will go with MY enforcers. The last thing we need is the ocean turning red with unnecessary bloodshed. Your enforcers are nothing but barbarians!"

Rass feinted hostility as Halfar commanded he do so in these situations. Kur gave a smirk and strolled pass him in triumph. Rass sighed with relief and shut the double doors to the throne room.

"Now that he is gone, how fares your pregnant mate?"

Chardon ate like a manbeast after battle just to keep her appetite at bay. She was not happy with the amount of food even though she knew it was necessary. Her time was near, she was due to deliver soon. Jaron had been around earlier to help with preparations. For some reason she did not feel strange or uneasy as everyone said she would be. Then, again, Chardon was not like the others of her race. That's why she was leader. Her strength and power were unmatched; it was her emotional state that made her weak at times.

"Feeling better, I see."

She noticed Ganna going over to the bed to straighten out the covers. The scientist had not left Chardon alone all day. She kept coming in unannounced to check on her.

"I've been eating."

Chardon shoved another piece of grilled meat in her mouth.

"That's good, you will need all the energy you can muster."

"Really? I was under the impression my being conscious was not necessary since you plan to cut him out of me."

Ganna paused mid cleaning and didn't dare look over her shoulder at Chardon. It was an option she had floated around only to receive instant resistance from Halfar and the medical workers She would still do it if she could get away with it.

The scientist in her called for it.

"It would have been an evasive procedure that you would not have gotten away with."

Ganna flinched, satisfying Chardon with her reaction.

Halfar barely made it back in time to see the bloody slimy mess of child birth occurring in Chardon's chamber with at least five other witnesses packed in. Coming around to the foot of the bed, he saw Ganna gently pulling out a gelatinous membrane encased around a tiny life with equally tiny black talons. The sounds of it coming out reminded him of the last time he accidently stepped on fresh entrails during a battle.

The membrane was set in a large bowl at the foot of the bed and Ganna carefully sliced it open to reveal the child. Laying the filleted membrane open faced, she dug into his mouth and nostrils with her fingers and extracted the protective tissue simultaneously.

A high-pitched wail filled the room and he swiped at her, his tiny razor-sharp talons grazing her cheek leaving three thin lines of blood. She picked him up and went to the wash basin to clean him off. One of the medical workers handed her a small blanket to wrap him in.

"Here he is." Ganna gave the little monster to Chardon then went to the mirror to examine her face.

Chardon reached into a basket near the head of her bed and palmed a handful of bandage cloth.

"Help me." She motioned to Halfar.

Together they loosely bound up his tiny claws so no one else would get sliced open. After that was done, she hoisted him up high by his under arms for inspection. The tiny slits of his eyes opened, and he stared at her with the same strange green as his father.

His hair was black as pitch with honey brown streaks the color of Chardon's. She handed their child over to him and he was frightened to hold him.

"What shall we name him?" He asked her as his eyes laid transfixed on his son, mewing and clicking sounds bubbly from his tiny lips.

Lending a finger, he watched the little one take hold and open his mouth. A row of sharp tiny teeth was exposed and before Halfar could snatch his finger back, the little one chomped down. Droplets of blood formed around it.

Seeing that, Chardon decided.

"His name will be Farin."

"That's quite appropriate." Jaron snorted. "It means feral fangs in our culture."

Halfar smiled at that. He liked how it fit him perfectly. Farin let go of the finger, yawned, then shivered.

"He's cold."

Chardon tossed the blanket to him and Halfar wrapped him back in it. Farin warmed up after only a few minutes and fell asleep.

"How sweet he is for such a creature." Ganna mused to herself.

Her face froze realizing she had said it out loud. She winced when silence filled the room.

Halfar knew how she felt about manbeasts, or similar species, and frowned. Jaron seemed to feel the same as he did and also not amused by Ganna's remark. Just because a child is born with talons does not make them a monster. She went over to take a peek at the sleeping Farin being held in Halfar's arms.

"He's quite cute like a baby manbeast without the fur," she said glaring over at Ganna.

A small blue light flashed on the back of Halfar's hand, signaling his time was up for now. He struggled with his emotions of wanting to stay at Chardon's side or go back to deal with Earth once and for all.

Standing, he handed the sleeping bundle to Chardon, kissing them both on the forehead before grabbing his cloak and heading out the door. Rass would cover for him always. It was getting harder to go back and forth while Kur lurked in the shadows waiting for an opportunity to finish them both off. Ahead, he saw Modas opening the gate for his return.

"This won't be necessary for much longer," he told the manbeast as he stepped onto the platform. "We can go over strategy soon."

Modas' fingers worked the console as he replied.

"We will help get you off Earth." He looked up from his work. "You have to deal with Kur on your own."

"You're right."

Halfar entered the vortex and disappeared.

FOUR:

Ready to Strike

Rass moved the remains of his meal around on the plate in front of him, not having much of an appetite anymore. The great dining hall table had a capacity to seat fifty. Today only his lord and he were present. It too was pure white from floor to ceiling. Two servants stood in wait on opposite sides of the room to serve them. Halfar sat across from him, twenty feet away, on the other end of the table after just informing him of what needed to be done about Kur. Something about it pained him and he didn't like the way he was feeling.

"Can you do it?" Halfar asked urgently.

Rass was surprised he had been ignoring Halfar. He had not heard anything his ruler said after the instructions.

"You have asked me that even before this and the answer is still yes."

"Then why are you not enthused about it?"

"As you've said, I was in love with him once."

"Are you still? Do you think he will miraculously change?"

Rass tossed the fork down onto the plate and sat back in the chair sideways.

"I am not a fool, no." He squinted in aggravation at the thought of Kur. "He has made it clear I am not ideal."

"You really should find a mate soon. I worry about you."

"Hmm? This, coming from our ruthless ruler who decided to fall in love after centuries of conquests? I'll have you know, battles are what drive me, not love. Besides," he put his feet up on the edge of the table, "How can I be an objective General, all lovelorn and what not?"

More servants came in to clear away the table and Halfar noticed the half-eaten food on Rass' plate.

"Not hungry this evening?"

"Earth food is disgusting."

"You do get quite the variety."

Kur burst into the dining hall with all the flair of an entertainer.

"How fares my lord and his minion?"

He did a quick bow, smirking as he came up to the edge of the table. His sing song introduction grated on both their sensibilities.

"Did you come for dinner?" Rass motioned to the spread of food being taken away. "We are finished but there is plenty left for you."

Kur crinkled his nose. "Disgusting." He came further into the room and made his report. "I have secured the Asian border, so they will not be a problem for our forces." The emphasis on 'I' was noticed. "By the way, when is the Armada coming down to raze the surface?"

"Once we are all in position for a unified attack. I believe we are at forty percent?"

"Oh," was all Kur could muster as an answer.

Rass could see him thinking about it. It did make sense and he would just had to wait a little longer for his plan to ambush Halfar during the attacks.

"Yes, that is correct. Rest assured, we will be ready on schedule." He bowed and exited.

Halfar drummed his fingers on the arm rests. He knew exactly what Kur was thinking and it gave him all the more reason to unleash Rass on him when the time came.

Locking eyes with Rass on the other end, he nodded. Rass stood and bowed out as well to make his own battle plans. Alone in the dining hall, Halfar leaned back and thought of his new born son.

A smile crept on his face. Farin being his first child, he couldn't figure out why it had taken him so long to understand the meaning of procreation. A century of frolicking produced none because he made sure it did not. Child rearing was the last thing on his agenda.

Until now.

Farin could be vicious when provoked. That didn't stop Ganna from trying to take him for some extra testing of his biological system. While the guardians at the sandbox were preoccupied, Ganna snuck in and snatched the sleeping infant without disturbing the other baby beasts.

She paid for it dearly when he woke up as they entered the lab and bit into her arm, the swiping motion of his head opening a nasty gash in her flesh. That is how Chardon found her in the search for her son; Ganna bleeding profusely cursing the infant as she tossed him aside against a nearby table to tend her wounds.

"You little monster! I'd dissect you if I thought no one would miss you."

She had the sealing tool in her hands when she turned and saw Mara, with Chardon, standing in the doorway. Immersed in her own treatment, she had not seen them enter the medical chamber. There was a simmering of malice in both their eyes that left Ganna cold inside. She smiled sweetly.

"Chardon! I was going to find you later. I needed to do a check up on your little one, so I brought him here." Their expressions did not change.

Mara went around Chardon and retrieved Farin. With him safely in her arms, she left the chamber. Whatever was about to happen, she wanted no part of. Ganna felt she may have gone too far this time.

"I would like to think you were blinded by some sick sense of scientific discovery. Knowing how you really feel about manbeasts and my child, who is similar, I believe you have an intense hatred for them." Chardon stepped closer to her. "You made an error. That child you are so intent on dissecting is MY child."

She grabbed Ganna by the neck with lightning speed and picked her up from the floor. Ganna gagged dropping the sealing tool. Blood dripped onto the floor below creating a small pool. With the other hand, Chardon was in the process of forming an energy ball.

"Stop!"

Jaron flew into the room and knocked Ganna out of Chardon's grip. Her body landed against an operating table and she slid down, touching her neck.

"She is not worth it!" Jaron pulled Chardon away, leaving Ganna to herself. "Come away!"

As they left the chamber, not bothering to shut the door, and into the clearing, Chardon whirled on Jaron who was ready to defend herself.

"Why did you stop me?" she seethed calmly.

"Because, we don't need to explain the death of our lead medical healer. Whether you like it or not, we still need her."

"She is no better than Sestis."

Jaron's head snapped upward.

"What do you mean?" Chardon turned away from her and headed for the sandbox. "She couldn't have! Chardon!"

She went after her almost running.

Ganna crawled over to the sealing tool and used it to close her wound. Hearing the way Jaron yelled in surprise, she figured Chardon would have to tell her about Sestis.

Can't keep all your secrets hidden much longer, leader.

Jakar always had his little siblings to play with. When Mara came in, Farin in tow, he couldn't help taking him up for inspection. He frowned at the bandaged up tiny hands.

Was that really necessary?

They stared at each other silently for a long time making it a peculiar sight when Jaron and Chardon walked in. It was probably endearing, if he could say so himself.

"Bonding with your new cousin?" Chardon asked.

His mother shook her head in warning as she went to check on Trinon asleep in the sandbox.

"He is quite vicious so be careful." Jakar frown at that and glance at her with doubt. "Just ask Ganna. She's probably in the process of sealing that wound he gave her."

He looked back at Farin with admiration.

"You didn't do anything drastic, right?" Mara asked.

"Your mother stopped me."

"I am relieved. I never knew she was capable of something like that. Does she feel that way towards manbeasts too?"

"Yes, she does." Jaron replied. "She hides it well enough for most. I knew long ago what she really thought and of me, who mated with one."

Bringing Farin back down, Jakar handed him over to Chardon.

"He does smell of blood."

Mara leaned over him to check again to make sure she had not missed any.

"I rinsed his mouth out with some of the spring's water. He ended up swallowing some of it though."

Seeing Trinon was indeed comfortable, His mother left, probably to find his father. He could tell by her expression that she must have found out more about Sestis and her disturbing deeds.

Was everything their race had endured really all leading up to her actions?

As angry as he was with Talas and Kelin, it was clear they were merely gears in a giant machine.

Modas was meditating by the waterfall near the mountains so Jaron approached him quietly in vain. He opened his eyes and glanced over at her. The look on her face told him whatever she wanted was serious enough to need his undivided attention.

He didn't stand up, just motioned for her to sit in front of him.

"Ganna decided in her infinite wisdom to snatch Farin from the sandbox and do some experimenting. Chardon went to the medical lab and was about to murder the conniving scientist. I had to stop her."

Modas shifted uneasily on the slab of rock. He too knew about Ganna's obsession with dissecting manbeast like creatures for her scientific research.

"Chardon had hinted about Sestis' role in torture. I have some theories on what they could have entailed. You know something, don't you? Why won't you tell me?"

"Would it matter?"

"Stop keeping secrets from me! You and Chardon always have something only the two of you know. Why is that? Tell me!"

He sighed and cleared his throat.

"She had a thing for learning how other species

functioned. Her and Ganna devised ways to 'procure' specimens. It came to a head when Sestis learned of Chardon and Halfar's affair. She threatened to expose them. I decided to protect them from her and she turned on me."

"What?" Jaron reared back.

✦✧✦

Lassa: Over 100 Years Ago

Modas watched from the chamber door cracked slightly open as Sestis admired herself in the seven-foot viewing glass she had brought back from one of her inter-planetary meetings. She was quite beautiful with chestnut colored curls kept piled high on her head and deep blue eyes. Her pale skin had a sheen to it, giving the illusion she glowed. At a little over six feet tall, she was statuesque.

The door made a loud creaking sound as Modas entered her private chamber, causing her to look towards it. She turned, moving the bottom of her golden embroidered robe out of the way. No one on their planet dressed as such so it made her stand out. She had said it made her feel regal whenever she wore it. Some seedy merchant on one of her many well solicited planet excursions had it made for her in exchange for company.

"Come for a mid-evening tryst with your leader?"

Her smile was wide and sinister.

"You are not my leader."

"Really? Because I am the one who rules this world, not Chardon."

"Our world has no ruler. This is not a dictatorship."

"I beg to differ, you monster!" She leaned on the banister attached to the viewing glass. "Because of me our reach spans across the galaxy."

"That is not what we wished for. We want to be left alone. If the people knew…"

"What? That their leader is a changeling mating with some disgusting off world creature? I could expose that truth!"

"No. I will tell them about you."

"You will do no such thing, manbeast!" She hissed then laughed. "If you so much as attempt to speak one word I will have you torn apart by a Razznian, your body parts tossed into the meat pile for processing. How would your mate like the taste of her beloved manbeast roasted with herbs?"

Modas moved towards her. She was quicker and rammed him into the wall, pinning him there. Tendrils of energy writhed around his neck from her fingertips.

"You are not special, monster. Chardon will be obedient and so shall you. Are we in agreement?"

"Understood."

She released him and waved her hand, signaling him to leave. He left to check on Chardon who no doubt had a similar run in with her.

Jaron was more upset by this revelation than she thought she would be from the outcome of his explanation. If Sestis were alive today, she would kill her herself. The manipulation she had engaged in was counterproductive to their race. Their race! Jaron recalled what Halfar said about trying to repair the damage caused by her with the interplanetary councils.

"What has she done? We don't want interference from other races. Are we now considered some galactic power?"

"Not anymore because as far as the councils know, our race was destroyed. We no longer exist."

Thinking of the implications of that, Jaron put her hands to her face and gasped. No one knew of their settlement on this planet. There was obviously no help coming and why their resources were so low. She stared at her mate and they both silently agreed once and for all to help Halfar instead of double crossing him as planned.

"We need to find out how to open the gate to the other worlds." Jaron suggested.

"Halfar knows how to access them."

"Can we really fix what she has done?"

"All we can do is try."

Chardon sat in her chamber breast feeding Farin, his tiny claws latched into her flesh. This was the only time she unwrapped his hands. Because her skin healed fast, it was of no concern. He gurgled and kept on drinking.

She was amazed he never cried and stared at everyone with such conviction, as if analyzing them. Chardon did not want to be overly protective after the incident with Ganna. She had to consider a guardian for him. Maybe Mara or Und would be willing to take on the task.

The gate opened at the far edge of the fields and Halfar hurried through the vortex and onto the planet's soil. He nodded at the guardian and walked hastily towards the housing commons to see his son. His stride slowed as he reached the entrance. Entering Chardon's chamber seeing mother and child silently sitting on the bed, Farin asleep with his claws still hooked into his mother's breast, made his chest tighten.

"I never thought you could be any more beautiful than before, yet you are."

"Don't start with that. I'm trying to keep him from waking up."

Halfar raised an eyebrow at what she was implying. Mating would be a great release for the anxiety he had pent up inside.

"That is not what I came for." He sat down next to her and kissed her shoulder, careful not to jostle Farin. "Maybe another time. He's sweet." Halfar blurted out. "It must be from your race."

"He's also vile when he attacks." Halfar leaned away, curious. "Ganna snatched him while he was asleep, so he bit a chunk out of her. All for her research, I suppose."

"Shall I give her what she wants and dissect her instead?" He was furious, deciding to remain calm. "I had a feeling she was up to something sinister when she suggested slicing you open to retrieve Farin."

"I wanted to murder her right then and there. Jaron stopped me."

"Your cousin is more level headed than you think, because she was correct."

Chardon turned to him. "How did you know we were cousins?"

"Because, I asked long ago why your names were so similar. Modas speaks when he wants to."

"Ahh. Well our parents were not very original when it came to that."

Halfar tucked his hands gently under Farin and pulled him off her, cradling him in his arms. He didn't stir as his father laid back on the bed with him.

"I want to stay."

"Then stay." Chardon crawled onto the bed to lay next to him.

"I can't, not yet. Not until this is done."

"Then get it done, quickly."

☼

"Don't treat me like baby!" Trinon snapped at Mota.

Some of the warriors still in the battle arena hurriedly grabbed their gear and exited into the surrounding fields. Domestic quarreling between manbeasts could get ugly.

"You need to let your hands heal!"

Mota flicked him in the forehead. He had found his little brother at the training site for combat maneuvers learning to use his legs and feet in a fight. Trying to keep Trinon in one place for more than an hour was proving to be a challenge. At the same time, he knew getting back on schedule was a good thing for him. On instinct, Trinon punched him in the stomach with both fists and regretted it. The pain made him suck in too much air and he swooned. Mota caught him and let him struggle.

"Please, just rest for the day." He felt Trinon slump and little hands wrapped around him.

Not far from them, Modas and Jakar stood watching the two brothers bond. They were unclear if Mota would be a hindrance or an asset to the coming mission. His demeanor suggested a mind too soft for combat except they both knew he could snap out of it at any moment and be just as deadly as any other warrior.

"If you need me to deal with Kur, let me know." Jakar offered.

"No need. Halfar will take care of that."

"Then I can focus on the enforcers stationed near North America."

"Just be careful. Those enforcers are not normal, as Halfar explained."

"Not to worry," Mara came up behind them, "I will back up the old one." Jakar made a face. "Yes, I am referring to you, and not our father." She flung an arm over each of their shoulders and focused on what they were observing. "Ahh, that makes me wish I were still a little one. You were so nice to me then."

"I still am."

Jakar grabbed her arm off his shoulder and flipped her over, even though she had not let go of their father. He came tumbling down as well to one knee. Jakar made no apologies to either as he stepped away from them.

"Father, sister." With that, he walked off.

"See? Even you get sucked into his ill manners." Mara brushed dirt off her robes.

Modas, still on bended knee started to smile a little then a chuckle came out of him. Mara's eyes went wide with disbelief. She saw her mother in the distance and beckoned her.

"Come quickly! Look!" Jaron tripped as she neared them seeing the silent giant, Modas, having a brief laugh at his children's expense. "He's actually laughing!"

He stopped and made a serious face as he stood to tower over his mate.

"That was not a laugh."

"Oh, it was." Jaron grinned. She jabbed him in the rib. "You should do it more often."

Halfar watched the holoscreen floating in front of him while he marched towards the center of the palace with his personal army in tow. Arriving, he made sure his entourage was securely positioned in the circle carved on the floor. The entire outer ring rotated around making the center ascend to the ceiling opening above. Wind swirled down through it like a tornado as it gaped wider to let the platform through. He took his attention from the holoscreen to look up. It was about to begin.

From information leaked purposely by Rass, the military Earth forces created a unified front to engage the enemy. Makeshift underground bunkers had been made to evacuate as many civilians as possible while military guarded encampments popped up in regions furthest away from the warzones for those refusing to go under and face their fate head on. He found that part rather asinine on the humans' part. There was an eerie silence around the world.

Rass relayed orders to his troops via commlink as well as to Halfar. He sent the one recruited by Kur in his plan to kill Halfar to a hostile region heavily armed by Earth forces. It would be a slaughter. Another troop he positioned to lay in wait for Kur's third wave on the Asian border.

Once Jakar arrived through the vortex, they would rendezvous with Earth's military forces to destroy Kur's modified enforcers. Rass would command the remaining troop himself to Kur's location off the southern coastline of North America. This time, he won't hold back his power. Kur deserved nothing less.

Since Halfar was never unguarded on a battlefield, Kur had to make sure he separated him from the main force midway in the melee and make it seem like an accident. He was not to be positioned anywhere near Halfar's troops, except his plan demanded it. A lowly enforcer was no match for their ruler. His main army would be elsewhere while four enforcers and himself blended into Halfar's army.

He smiled at the brilliance of his plan. Soon, the cherished almighty Armada would be his to command. His smile faded remembering Rass, also a General in line to take the reins. The smile returned. He would get rid of that one too. Checking the number of modified enforcers under his command, he was satisfied he could win.

"Come, my warriors! Let us strip this planet to its core and see what lies beneath!"

Mota used his teeth to tighten the leather strips around his wrists, flexing his fingers to make sure they had ample movement. Trinon watched him from a seat directly below him. The sandbox was empty due to Chardon implementing a state of isolation. It was a precaution just in case the enemy somehow got through one of the gates. Sighing, Mota looked down at him.

"Well, I guess I'm off to rid Earth of some nasty enforcers."

"You'll be right back?" Trinon asked in barely a whisper.

"Of course I am!" Mota threw his head back and laughed loudly, suddenly stopping short as he noticed Trinon was not amused. The little one just sat with a downward stare. "Look at me." Trinon obeyed. "There is nothing that would stop me from coming back."

"Except death."

"I am not dying on that miserable rock and neither is anyone else. Understood?" Trinon nodded. "Good!" He bent down and ran his fingers through Trinon's mane. "No training until I get back."

Jakar startled them out of their moment. He waited for Mota to join him at the edge of the field and they left together.

"It's time."

Battle Cries

At the gate console, a small army of energy users and manbeasts were lined up in groups ready to deploy. There were nine groups in all, the main one being the largest, which included Chardon and Modas. Back in male form, Chardon was ready for battle. Jaron, Jakar, Talas, Kelin and four other warriors led a group for the assault. The army was small enough to maneuver the landscape unnoticed yet deadly enough to cause major damage to the enforcers without any casualties of their own. Talas planned to keep his promise.

Chardon went over the rendezvous points for each group via holoscreen while Ganna input coordinates on the gate console. A virtual map of Earth's entire planet surface was floating in midair on display. The whole operation was going to be tricky since Earth defense forces had no idea they were getting assistance from them. He shut down the holoscreen in front of him with a wave of his hand and turned to Modas.

"I don't have to stress that we get in, get out and sever the entrance to that planet forever."

"No." Modas flexed his fingers.

He was itching for another fight with the enforcers.

"Do we really have to close it for good?" Ganna addressed them. "We could do some business with them. Maybe even help them with repairs in exchange for…"

Chardon did not let her finish.

"We will no longer interfere with that planet and its people. They are not ready and won't be for at least another century."

"I think gauging their readiness is premature..." Ganna started.

"Someone else had the same theory and look where it got us."

There was deafening silence as all knew who he meant. Ganna frowned and returned to her duties of opening multiple vortexes. Chardon did not trust her. He motioned to Jaron signaling her to hurry with Talas' backup plan. There was no need. He noticed Talas had seen the look on Ganna's face and already moving the timetable up in his head.

The first vortex opened for Kelin's group to arrive on the European front. He bowed to Talas then led the way through. Next was Jakar and Mota to the Asian border. Every group went in sequence as planned with Chardon's being the last to arrive in the North American region. They would rendezvous with Halfar's troops hoping he had a plan to defeat Kur. He was the last person they wanted to deal with on the battlefield.

From the command deck on the armada's mother ship, Halfar watched cities burn across the planet called Earth. He wished it had not been. Too late now. This was something Kur put into motion and had to be seen to the end.

The council members, who had backed Kur on his little plan to send his armada, were executed when found on the ship. They apparently wanted front row viewing of the massacre and proof of Halfar's demise. That was why he hated politics of any kind. Not once, did his now former council think to poll the inhabitants of their world to see if they were dissatisfied with his as ruler, which he knew was not the case.

Punching in coordinates, he saw something peculiar. Kur's signature was not with his forces off the southern coast. Instead, it showed he was near the rear of Halfar's army on the Northern border near Canada. Kur would not have noticed Halfar missing at the front due to it being heavily guarded as if he were. Although it disturbed him how far his general was taking this, he grinned and relayed a message to Rass.

"How clever of you," he spoke to the blinking red dot representing Kur on the screen.

Newly devised and barely tested weaponry was being rolled out against the alien enforcers and seemed fairly effective at holding them back. Jaron was almost proud of the humans, the sentiment squashed knowing those same weapons would be turned on each other sometime after this battle died down. Humans were a double-edged mystery to her.

As both sides retreated from the other, she made small explosions with her energy spheres to coax the enforcers into an isolated area away from the Earth forces' view. Once there, her group went into a full assault.

The Asian front was a lesson in brutality and strict methods as Jakar witnessed the streamlined attacks from their defense forces. Had he known humans were capable of this, he would have brought fewer warriors.

Nonetheless, he needed Mota to draw the enemy away from the Earth people and into their combat zone. To do that, an immediate threat had to be present. He was able to lure the enforcers to an opening in the Asian forces and waited for them to retreat. It worked. Jakar's group came up from behind the enforcers and took them down from there.

Chardon was having a hard time trying to keep the Earth defense forces in his region from assisting. His group had been noticed and after the human in command decided they were friend not foe attempted to negotiate. He explained to the commanding officer who he was and why his race was helping yet the man insisted they defend their own planet. He was right. Still, Chardon knew they were no match for the enforcers Kur dispatched. It was also dangerous because when Chardon unleashed a ball of energy, it decimated a large chunk of the area. There was no discrimination within its path.

Modas made it no better carving gashes into the air as he sliced up nearby enforcers. There were too many and that seemed odd. He landed from one of his high jump assaults next to Chardon and they stood back to back. Even the humans could see there was a huge disproportionate number of enforcers for this area. Something was amiss. Chardon realized it almost instantly.

"Kur is keeping us busy for a reason."

"He is not here, but his army is."

"Halfar." Chardon had a feeling this might happen. "Let's get this cleaned up." He turned to the commanding officer. "Are you ready?" He scanned over the dead and wounded spread across the battle ground. The commander nodded. "Good. Here we go."

Halfar had seen enough from the view station of the mother ship's command center. To set up such an unbalanced battle for the sole purpose of mass slaughter was a bit much for his taste. He liked being on equal ground in a fight. If it was a battle Kur wanted, then that is what he will get.

Rounding up a few more soldiers, he headed to the transport room. No matter what the consequences, he wanted to keep Chardon from harm. He had no faith in the manbeast's abilities to do so.

A bright red beam the color of blood shot down from the sky and hit the planet surface near the advancing forces in the Northern region of the Americas. On impact, a two-mile radius of infrastructure and everything in its vicinity was destroyed. The beam waned until disappearing, in its place Halfar and his personal guards stood. They marched to intercede with his forces ahead, paying no attention to the debris left in their wake.

The front guards opened to allow Halfar and his entourage into the fold and reclosed ranks, strengthening their formation. As it moved forward, they were receded further back into the lines until Halfar and his guards were in the middle, protected on all sides. Which didn't go unnoticed by the rear guards some three miles away.

Kur could not believe what he had just witnessed. It never occurred to him Halfar was not commanding his own army. His rage hit a whole new level and he thought of tearing his ruler's body apart instead of just the quick death blow he had planned. The battle still in the beginning stages, he felt it was the perfect time to be rid of him. Signaling his small group of enforcers who had infiltrated Halfar's army with him to step out of ranks they headed into position.

Up ahead, a vortex opened in front of Halfar's army letting Rass and a handful of his enforcers through. He wasted no time in rushing towards the middle to grab hold of Halfar and pull him out. On his side view he could see Kur advancing from the rear.

"What are you doing?" Halfar was about to break free.

"Did you not command me to deal with Kur myself?" Rass was desperate and angry.

Halfar jolted still and raised his head to Rass who made sure to convey his frustration and rage in his stare. It seemed in his rush to deal with Kur his ruler had forgotten that part of the plan. Chardon and Modas were capable of defeating the army of enforcers against them. Halfar had let his emotions get the better of him.

"Then do it!"

Rass did the unthinkable in front of his ruler's army. He threw Halfar behind him and into the vortex leading to Chardon's location. It closed shut right when Kur came through the middle of the formation, cutting down enforcers as he advanced. At the clearing he nearly ran into Rass who stood waiting for him.

"Disappointed?" Rass cocked his head to one side. When Kur sneered, he went into an attack stance.

Kur laughed.

"Are you going to stop me? You can't defeat me."

A vortex opened behind him and more enforcers spewed out unleashing death on the unsuspecting army. Rass called out an order to have the remaining forces regroup away from the vortex as it closed. Kur smiled.

"My victory is secure and when I am through with you I will go after Halfar and kill him as well!" He jumped backwards five hundred feet to let his enforcers charge Rass.

Rass was quite calm and didn't move an inch until the first wave of enforcers were in his perimeter. His whole body lit up with a red glow and with one swipe of his arm, a giant arc of red haze from his longsword sliced through them. Black blood flew in all directions sizzling as it landed on the ground.

The second wave stopped advancing. Kur stood in shock behind them while Rass repositioned himself back into his attack mode, his long sword back behind him.

Pieces of his enforcers rained down around Kur as he stared at Rass. This was not the same easily unhinged, ragtag soldier he had been provoking and manipulating the past few decades. No, this was something far more dangerous. It occurred to him that Rass had been holding back all this time.

That angered him even more, solidifying his resolve.

"There is no need for me to hold back then?" He questioned Rass. The other did not answer or move. "Very well." He drew his claws to their full length. "I'll make this quick."

It unnerved him when Rass did not have any clever jokes or got angry, making him unsure in his ability to defeat him in one blow. He leapt towards him.

A flash of light signaled the impact of their claws ramming into each other. Rass used the back of his legs to push upward into Kur's body and sent him flying with a small gash in his torso. As Kur landed, some of his enforcers moved to defend.

"No! Do not interfere!"

He looked to Rass. That same blank expression remained.

Had I been wrong all this time? Could I have mated with him to produce powerful warriors?

"Why won't you say anything?" he demanded.

"There's no need."

Rass was by his side with lightning speed and it took all of Kur's strength to torque his body out of range avoiding a fatal blow. He could see Rass mentally dying inside, having no choice and not let any emotions get in the way of defeat. Just as Kur cleared himself, Rass attacked him again from behind. One of his claws ripped through the back of his shoulder blade and exited out his chest in the front. He was going to go deeper and severe the entire arm. Kur spun around and pushed off him.

Bleeding and breathing heavily, Kur held his arm together and forced the wound to congeal shut, stopping the blood flow. Even from a distance he could see the hurt in Rass' eyes. It went away as they stared at each other, the blankness returned.

"Don't you see? Halfar is making you suffer by doing this because he's a coward who refuses to face me."

Rass tried not to frown, the struggle showing on his face. He was not going to be manipulated this way and Kur understood that the moment Rass let his guard down, Kur would strike and that would be his end. Rass raised his claws and resumed his attack stance. One death blow was all he needed to land, and Kur would be no more. He watched Rass' claws start to shake.

At that moment, Kur realized that he could not win this battle. The council had coerced him into this plan and were probably laughing at how foolish he was; here about to die at the hands of someone who once loved him, on a battlefield of his own doing.

He dropped to his knees and rose his head to the blackened sky scorched with red, not able to remember why he had come to this planet for conquest and why he had involved Halfar. Ah, yes. The council wanted a foothold in an uncategorized solar system. It was a random judgment and was now costing them everything.

Rass had not made his move yet when a vortex opened behind him, and from above, a body shot out and struck Kur where he knelt on the ground. Blood gurgled up and a strangled sound came from his lips as he heard Rass screaming. It took him a moment to realize what it was.

"NO!"

The manbeast, Modas stood towering over him. Removing his claws out of Kur's flesh, he turned a puzzled look towards Rass. Distraught, Rass came at him, knocking him out of the way. Kur's vision faded just as he felt Rass' arms wrap around him.

Halfar came out of the vortex and saw the tragic scene. He had a suspicion that Rass could not do it. Just as he regretted the destruction of Lassa and almost losing Chardon, he knew Rass was not capable of killing the one he loved.

It made it all the worse when he saw Rass snap his head around to face him and scream, "Why?" He had Kur's body hanging like a ragdoll in his arms.

"I'm sorry."

Halfar motioned his army to regroup with a signal of his hand and they commenced to destroying all of Kur's modified enforcers. It was like hell on Earth tenfold. The sounds, scents and black blood everywhere would make even the most fanatic of gore cringe.

"Can you get him to your healers?" He asked Modas, gesturing to Kur.

"What for?" Modas was not amused. His talons flexed.

Chardon stepped onto the battlefield taking in the horrors of the scene. This was too much to bear.

"Take him to Ganna!" Modas frowned at him. "Now!"

Modas complied by plucking Kur's body from Rass' arms and jumping into the vortex. Chardon went over to Rass and literally dragged him through the vortex, Halfar in tow.

"Was that really necessary?" Chardon referred to the massacre going on behind them.

"Believe me, it is. Those things were never meant to be.

Whoever authorized it will have me to deal with shortly."

"The Armada?"

"I left orders to depart as soon as the modified enforcers' numbers reach zero."

"Very thorough." Chardon closed the vortex. Modas would have to go through three more to arrive back on their world. "What about Rass?" They both looked down at the catatonic general. His limbs dangled like rubber from his body, eyes in a blank stare.

"He can recuperate on New Lassa before I send him back to our world as the leader for my armada."

"New Lassa? Did I say we were staying on that world?"

"I said I would fix it."

"Hmmm." He nodded towards Rass. "What makes you think he will obey you this time?"

"I have my reasons. He will be just fine. Plus," He smiled wickedly, "this will give him a chance to nurse Kur back to health." Charon shook his head in disbelief.

Mara heard the cheering and cries of relief as she led her small group out of the vicinity littered with pieces of modified enforcers. They had successfully rid the area of them without getting noticed by the Earth forces who were engaged in the battle. She made sure that her group somehow blended in, so no one was the wiser. Thinking of the clean up almost made her gag. She did not envy the humans for that task. Finding an inauspicious corner off the battlefield, she opened a vortex that led back to their world. Her mission was done.

The same was true of the other sites as humans celebrated their triumph over the alien enemy unaware that it was an internal fight between two alien factions and had nothing to do with them. Chardon returned to the Northern region to remind the Earth forces commander and his men not to tell a soul about how they were helped by an alien race. It would just complicate things. He watched the humans, too tired to celebrate, start to pack up their gear and move out. Whether they kept the promise or not was of no concern since the gate would be sealed for eternity.

Halfar returned to the mother ship and assessed the data on all modified enforcers. When the counter reached zero, he ordered the remaining troops back to the ship and prepare for the trip back to their home world. He had some government tasks to deal with before going back to New Lassa. His scientists needed to assemble a planet bomb to inject life into the planet and another one for its weak sun. Seeing Farin was at the top of that list. That would have to wait.

Explanations

Kur could hardly move as he forced his body to obey him. Although healed, he could still feel his wounds. He watched Ganna for a moment, immediately registering her as a threat. Ganna hummed to herself softly while examining the cultures she had collected from him before closing his wounds and reviving him.

Getting her hands on other races biological system made her juices flow. He was sure it had been a long time since she had access to such specimens. The last being when Sestis still lived.

So fascinated and engrossed in her studies, she did not hear Kur stirring on the operating table. She had not ordered his body moved to the recovery chamber. As he heard her explain, she planned on reopening him for more tests before Chardon came back.

Sitting further up until upright, he tried to extend a talon. The pain was excruciating, forcing him to hiss loudly which made Ganna jump out of her seat in fear. He saw her reach over to her right grasping for the weapon that lay near her fingers.

Chardon entered the chamber in female form. Kur could tell she had a feeling that Ganna was going to try something unsavory with him.

"And that will be enough. I believe your work is done. Why is he not in the recovery chamber?"

"I was waiting until he was stable."

Ganna moved her hand back, answering sweetly.

"That was not her intent!" Kur held his torso trying to breathe through pain. "Where am I?"

"A world we acquired after the destruction of our home world."

Kur made the connection from hazy memory.

"I always wondered why he kept your cores when he was the one responsible for your race's demise."

He swung his legs over the table and rested his head against the wall. He felt disoriented.

"There is someone who will be glad to see you are awake. I'll lead you to them."

"I can barely walk," he snapped, pushing himself off the wall to set his feet on the cold floor.

It became known to him that he was wearing his battle pants and nothing else as his body shivered. Chardon threw a long-sleeved robe at him along with some leather boots.

"You could use these, yes?"

As he dressed, he kept an eye on Ganna who stared at him with an unnatural lust. Not mating. What she wanted his body for made him dress quicker. Standing up, his vision blurred, and he barely caught himself with one hand bracing the wall. It finally cleared, letting him stand to his full height of seven feet.

Ganna pressed back into her desk. His slender frame must have deceived her into thinking he was smaller than Modas when in fact he was taller and menacing. It satisfied him a little to know she was afraid now.

"Come with me."

Chardon swept an arm towards the door at the same time giving Ganna a look of poison. If they did not need that woman, it would be so easy to rid themselves of her.

Mixed emotions swam around inside Kur's head when Chardon led him to a small living chamber with the bare minimum of furnishings. On the bed curled up in the fetal position was Rass looking small and vulnerable, unlike his usual self. His breathing seemed ragged and certain parts of his body twitched.

"What's wrong with him?" He whirled on Chardon, not sure why he was so angry.

"He's in a state of shock. Last time he saw you, you were presumed dead."

"I don't understand, he was ordered to kill me. Why would…?"

"Do you really think it would be easy for him to murder someone he holds dear even if they do not feel the same?" Chardon interrupted him. Kur's mouth clamped shut. "I will leave you alone. Surely, there is much to clarify."

She exited the chamber.

Kur moved slowly to the bed and eased as painlessly as he could next to Rass. Memories of how badly he treated him when they were still intimate so long ago filled his head. Hands shaking, he reached down and caressed his hair. Rass did not stir. Kur's chest began to hurt, and he lay across Rass' body to ease the pain. It should not have turned out this way.

☆

Battle scars were a cherished form of storytelling and it gave Mota a sigh of relief to see the wounds he received from the last battle disrupt the smooth new skin he had when revived. They made him feel whole again while he boasted about them to his young siblings. Und was not impressed and just stared disinterested at them. Trinon was inspecting each one with intensity and listening to every detail.

In the doorway stood Jakar watching the scene with the same look as Und. Bragging was a young manbeast's thing. After so many scars and battles it was just natural to forget about all that. With a sigh, he reached over and grabbed Mota by the mane, pulling him out of the commons onto the walk path with him.

"I was just getting to the best part!" "Hmm."

"You don't even have any! Your body is still pristine after getting your core back."

"I know how to not get hurt in a battle."

Mota was insulted, he could tell. His younger brother was just as good at fighting and he in no way was suggesting incompetence on the battle field.

"Maybe I don't avoid hand combat like some others." Jakar stopped walking, letting Mota know he had gone too far. "I don't mean that." He whispered.

"I should not have said that either."

Jakar resumed walking. They were already late for the debriefing with the council.

Chardon was already in talks with one of the agricultural engineers regarding the planet bomb meant to jump start the planet's growth. Halfar was coming through the gate as they spoke. The success of the mission was debatable. On the one hand, they were able to close the gate leading to Earth and on the other, Kur was not quite dealt with along with a handful of Halfar's advisors who managed to flee.

While Modas escorted Halfar, the two warriors conversed. The talk was strained, there being no amicable relation between them, though in their best interest considering their mates were related. As they neared the commons, Halfar slowed down.

"I want to see Farin."

"There's no time."

Modas kept his stride towards the council chamber. "We're late."

"Of course," Halfar let out a heavy breath of air. "Are your little ones well?"

"As could be."

"I heard one your sons had an accident during training."

"His claws were broken off."

It was said so nonchalantly that it did not register with Halfar at first. He halted.

"That is horrifying." It made him shudder.

"He heals fast." They had reached the outer door of the council chamber. "After you."

During the meeting, there were many opinions on what a good target for the planet bomb would be, from agriculture to natural resources. When it came down to the main factor, the sun and its lack of light and warmth, their focus on the matter took priority. This was much to the chagrin of the scientists, engineers and Ganna. Halfar turned the meeting over to his chief science officer who he brought with him from his home world, then signaled Chardon to leave with him.

Outside, they both walked up the short hill and through the fields to the commons where all the little ones congregated. Farin was now able to crawl a bit on his own. He never found out how far he could go because the older children often picked him up by his middle like a baby manbeast to play. Jaron had left the meeting early, so she was the culprit that grabbed him this time. As she raised him up she caught a glimpse of Chardon from the corner of her eye.

"Is the meeting over?"

"No. The scientists are going over strategy to do something about the sun."

"Oh." She turned her attention back to Farin. "Not interested."

"Can I have my child for a moment?" Halfar held out his arms. Jaron squinted at him then gave the little one up. "Thank you." He pulled Farin to him and smelled his skin.

"He's worse than a nursing maid." Jaron quipped, and Chardon whacked her in the back of her neck. "That was uncalled for!"

"I need to speak with Kur soon." Halfar said, his full attention still on Farin.

"I can take you to him. He may be a bit hostile."

"He's awake?" This was unexpected so soon.

"Ganna was going to take him back down and dissect him. Of course, she was going to reassemble and revive him."

"I'm sure she would have."

His sarcasm did not go unnoticed to Jaron who snorted.

Kur nor Rass had moved from their positions on the bed that barely held them. It was a strange sight for Halfar and he wasn't sure if disturbing them was a good idea. The way they were entangled together like two exhausted lovers made him regret asking Rass to rid them of Kur.

As much as he hated to do it, he went to the bed and jostled Kur awake. On reflex, Kur shot out an arm and grabbed Halfar by the wrist ready to toss him across the room. He found his prey would not budge from the weak pressure he had applied. Opening his eyes, he saw Halfar staring down at him with pursed lips. Bearing the pain in his body, he let go and eased up into a sitting position.

"My lord," He bowed his head glancing over at Rass.

"Don't wake him." A closer inspection made him notice Rass had not stirred, he turned to Chardon. "What's wrong with him?"

"This is your doing."

Kur sneered then averted his gaze.

"Is it? I am not the only one at fault."

"No, it isn't." Kur hung his head further down in defeat.

"Tell me why? What could you have possibly accomplished with this plan?"

"I was reassured by your advisors I would be given free reign over the armada and there were some hostile worlds needing to be conquered to expand our reach in the galaxy. I know now that Earth was picked at random because they were no real threat to us. It was to get rid of you all along. I was just a pawn to do the deed."

"Why get rid of me, the ruler of our world?"

"They told me that you planned to cede our home world to Razznians and they would control your armada."

"That's outrageous!" Halfar could not believe what he was hearing. "Where did such a lie come from?"

"With the invasion of Lassa, a deal was made to enslave the remaining population on Razzna in exchange for rulership over the Grata system which has seven planets."

"Who would be ruling that solar system?" Halfar was confused. Chardon had a sickening expression as she held her abdomen.

"That female Lassian, Sestis. The deal went south of course when the planet was not only scorched but destroyed with her on it. It was said that you brokered the deal with her since there were rumors you wanted her mate, Lassa's leader." He turned to Chardon making eye contact. "I figured they were right after seeing his obsessive behavior regarding your core."

"I would never…" Halfar was shaking with rage.

Sestis had set in motion more devastation than anyone thought. Chardon stood pale next to him.

"This is not over." Kur finally stood. "The Razznians will not be happy that her end of the deal was not fulfilled. With news that her race has survived and now on a new world, they will come after you."

"How long do we have?"

"Maybe ten years before they find this world and launch an assault."

Modas entered the chamber more silently than ever.

"We will be ready."

"I wish to redeem myself," Kur slid off the bed and knelt painfully down to one knee, "if it is your will."

"Stand up!" Halfar snapped. "We have something more serious than your redemption to consider!" He strolled up to Modas. "How many manbeasts are there, truly?"

"Enough. In ten years there will be nearly ten thousand."

Chardon tapped her lower lip and her eyes narrowed. "Sestis." Everything stemmed from her devious actions to gain power at the cost of her race. "Well, I guess we have to fight for our survival after all."

"This time, you will have my armada."

The news traveled quickly around the planet and soon everyone was preparing for a new battle. Months went by gathering knowledge for new technology and how to ration supplies. Halfar sent Kur and Rass to their home world to rectify the bizarre events that his former advisors had created.

A Rising

Trinon stood, now five feet ten inches tall, in front of the giant stone monolith looking up at the top of it. In silent admiration of its size, he unwrapped his hands letting the bandages fall on the ground. Without taking his eyes from the summit, he extended his talons, thicker and sharper than before from aging, and leapt high in the air.

He landed halfway up the stone wall and using his claws reached the top at an unimaginable speed neither out of breath or stamina. Satisfied, he did a back flip off the summit and sailed into the air laying back into the free fall with his eyes closed. The air concaved around him and his body's resistance felt good.

Mota, Jakar, Mara, and Und watched him from their position on a hill across form the monolith as he landed on the ground below in a kneeling position, his fist deep in the dirt. The impact caused a crater ten feet in diameter, and a few inches deep around him. He stood up straight, looking up at the summit again.

"I think he may be ready in five or ten years." Mota announced proudly.

"Or less," Modas added. Jakar nodded in agreement.

"I'll go spar with him." Und volunteered in a defeated tone.

"Oh, you won't get away that easy," Mota quipped. "You are just as ready."

Und smiled knowingly, his droopy lidded eyes holding a glimmer of excitement. He couldn't wait to get into a real fight alongside his siblings.

Excerpt from

SEEDS OF CONVICTION

CORE: BOOK TWO

BY MAQUEL A. JACOB

A Spy on Earth

The last alien warships ascended high above the charred remains of cities worldwide, into Earth's atmosphere. The battle between planet Azrom's rebel faction and Earth had come to a screeching halt with only a select few from each respective party knowing why. It was fierce and bloody with casualties disproportionate on the human's side. Somehow, every mutant Azrom enforcer had been wiped out. A mixture of relief and sorrow swept through the inhabitants of Earth.

The Razznian spy, dressed in a hooded track suit to hide the brown scaly skin covering his entire body, watched with curiosity as the humans struggled to comprehend the mass destruction left behind from a battle they had no idea how or why it started. His lidless red eyes scanned the area and his mouth opened to reveal two rows of razor sharp teeth, his equivalent of a smile. Observing, though not interacting with, the battle proved to be a good idea.

He had watched Azrom's armada supporting another alien group on the ground and upon getting a closer look, the Razznian realized they were Lassian; the race supposedly extinct by Azrom supreme ruler, Halfar's own hands.

How could they be here, and in such large numbers?

He made his way back to the rendezvous point where a portal sat open for his departure back to Razzna. He had a lot to report on.

Home Coming

The sky churned viciously as the Azromian Armada's mother ship descended from space at an angle through the stratosphere. All six thrusters rotated maneuvering beneath its underbelly in preparation for landing. The gunmetal hull covered with large spikes forced the air to concave around it as it emerged from the clouds. Correcting its position so it was perpendicular to the ground below, created winds with enough force to bend nearby trees nearly in half and rattle the palace's foundation.

Halfar watched, from the command center of the ship, as his palace guards rushed forward onto the roof to await his arrival. In full battle gear, he stood arms folded with his legs wide apart while the crew around him focused on controlling the ship. Being back on his home world sent a shiver through him. There was a lot of work to accomplish in order to rectify the damage done by his advisors, now deceased. He had dispatched them as a ruler was obligated to do.

The invasion and conquering of Earth, instigated by his advisors with General Kur as a scapegoat, turned into rescuing the human race from his own Armada. Assistance came from warriors of planet Lassa via their leader, Chardon. After the battle ended, the gate to Earth had been severed. Humankind was not ready for interaction with technologically advanced alien races.

More damage had been done to his soul and that of his men than anything else. The loss and regret spread wide over the Lassians, who he had nearly made extinct, and his own race. It was a mess he alone had to correct over the next few decades. Right now, he needed a plan for rebuilding his council and the trust of his generals.

With a roar and crushing winds, the ship settled into a hover over the palace platform. A small square of light opened at the underbelly and shot down a few hundred feet from the waiting entourage. The light rescinded and, in its place, stood Halfar with his two Generals, Rass and Kur, flanking him on each side followed by a handful of enforcers. Everyone's hair whipped into their faces as the ship moved laterally across the sky towards the docking bay located ten miles to the east.

The guards dropped down in unison to one knee, bowing their heads. Their left arm lay across the thigh while the other hand lay flat on the ground in front of them. Halfar grimaced at the display. It had been a long time since he witnessed the perfect triangular formation of his guards in full regalia. He glanced at Kur and saw the twinkle of delight in his eyes. Rass seemed unimpressed, for he didn't acknowledge the greeting. After a few moments, the guards stood back up and the leader came forward to address Halfar directly.

"My lord, it is good to see you again. It has been too long." He bowed his head again.

"Yes, a shame it has to be on these circumstances."

"Indeed."

The leader's face scrunched up as if he had smelled something rotten. Halfar motioned towards the door leading into the palace and the guards about faced, parting like the red sea to allow passage.

"How long will you be staying this time, my lord?" He had to try and keep his lord's fast pace while conversing.

"At the least, until I elect a new council and assure the progress of rebuilding."

As the entourage passed the guards at the palace entry, Halfar saw slight movement out of the corner of his eye and witnessed Rass attempt to stop himself from stumbling by reaching out to place his hand on a wall nearby. His physical injuries were minor. The mental anguish he suffered manifested as physical pain. Kur caught him by the elbow on impulse. It occurred in mere seconds and no one else noticed. He worried about both his young Generals.

The doors to the throne room were opened by two guards to reveal a massive hall built like a large cave made of golden Amber rock. Torches along the walls gave it a coppery glow. Giant columns the color of sandstone spaced twenty feet apart from each other stood majestic connecting to the ceiling. Entering the throne room, Halfar motioned for servants with his hand and twenty of them appeared lining up in two rows on either side of the hall.

He proceeded to his rightful seat, taking the stone steps two at a time, and turned to face the entrance before plopping down in a heap. Rass and Kur came up to take their place on either side of him. A servant advanced and Halfar waved him closer, whispering instructions in his ear. The servant stepped back, bowed low, and left the hall taking four other servants with him.

"My Lord, is there anything you require of your royal guards at this moment?"

The captain of the guard stood at attention in the entryway.

"No, keep watch of the gateway portal and wait for another arrival."

"My Lord?" The Captain raised one eyebrow.

"I have," Halfar hesitated for a moment. This was a delicate matter. "Acquired a mate."

There was a palpable silence as the news took hold. Halfar had never taken a mate before or had any interest in procreating for that matter. A mate now seemed a bit too sudden for them.

"She should be arriving two moons from now with a small group and," Halfar sighed heavily knowing this would be yet another shock, "my son." He heard the gasps.

"Congratulations, My Lord!" They all shouted in unison.

"A royal heir is to be celebrated," the Captain announced.

"Yes, yes. When they arrive, we will discuss the details." Halfar waved them away.

As the guards exited the throne room, the doors thundering shut, Kur turned to him and tsked. He was rewarded with a look of disgust complete with narrowed eyes.

"My Lord, divulging such matters on the first day is irresponsible of you. You could have at least waited a moon cycle to spring it."

"It would not have mattered either way."

The male servant from earlier returned with the other four carrying various trays of food and refreshments. Each tray was laid at the edge of the throne's platform. He carried two large cushions on top of his head for the two generals. It was not a moment too soon. Rass eased himself down onto the cushion set beside him and went into a near fetal position. Kur sat down cross legged on his and glanced over with a worried expression.

"Leave us," Halfar ordered. The other servants along the walls hesitated. He knew why. Their ruler should never be left unattended. Currently, he had no patience for it. "Now!"

He watched them all flee through the inner chamber doors on the far side of the hall.

Making sure the last one was far gone, Halfar pushed himself off his throne and crawled over to Rass. He checked his breathing by laying a hand on his chest to feel the rise and fall of it. Rass did not stir from the touch. Halfar saw Kur's shadow fall over them. Stealthy as ever. He brushed some of Rass' hair away from his face and stood up next to Kur. They both looked at each other; Halfar contemplating, Kur accusatory.

In the previous battle before their return, Halfar had given Rass the mission of eliminating Kur, who had acted in what he thought was treason. Knowing their past history as lovers, it must have seemed especially cruel given Kur's situation. The act in itself caused Rass to mentally break and Halfar knew he was to blame. The following months afterwards on the planet New Lassa found Kur trying to repair their damaged relationship.

"He is in no shape to deal with the reforming of the regiments." Kur stated the obvious.

"Then you have to deal with it along with inspection of the battle ships."

"That leaves you to do what, exactly?"

"Deal with the remaining council members who weren't stupid enough to go against me."

"Ahh, well I bid you success."

"First, we rest a bit." Halfar went back to his throne. "You will stay with him for a while after I leave?" Kur's face scrunched up as he turned to him. "Should I not have bothered to ask?" He eased back and began to contemplate how to rectify the damage done.

Assessments

Chardon surveyed the landscape of New Lassa for the best options to make it more habitable for his race. Their original home had been destroyed, scorched black, by a planet bomb sent from Halfar. An event regretted by all involved. Scientists from both races collaborated to find a remedy for the planet's weak sun and now in the works. A brighter sun meant more heat and better vegetation. So far, the highest temperature during the warm season reached a mere 21 degrees Celsius. The eyes of everyone on the planet over the past few decades started changing to accommodate its light.

Loud screeching from across the fields made Chardon's head snap up and turn towards the sound. It meant one thing; her son was being teased by one of the older man-beasts. She smiled at that. If not by Mota, then possibly Trinon. Both were the sons of her personal guardian, Modas. Soon, they would travel to Azrom to stay with her mate, Halfar, for a little while.

The visit was more like a war council than a family reunion. Chardon's previous mate, Sestis, had set into motion a string of events that threatened both Lassa and Azrom. Planning should only take a decade at most. The only way to battle their new joint enemy, Razzna, was to combine their forces and hope for victory. Razznians were a nasty species who fought with no sense of honor simply because they were not as strong as they appeared.

Off in the distance, a tall male figure advanced towards her. As he got closer she immediately knew who it was. His brown sandy colored mane hung down to the back of his knees, swaying in the light breeze. What started as a tiny smile grew, spreading across his angelic face as he caught sight of Chardon, steely blue eyes reflecting the sunlight. He was wearing a full tunic suit with the undone robe flapping around his six foot five inch muscled frame.

"Trinon," Chardon started to ask his question.

"Hmm?" Even at a distance, a manbeasts' hearing was impeccable.

"Was that you torturing my son earlier?"

Trinon's smile turned into a big wide grin. "No, not at all." He stopped a few feet from Chardon and his eyes averted away. All he had to do next was stick his tongue out and Chardon would have smacked him. It was something Trinon became fond of doing lately to appear innocent and cheeky.

"Really?" Chardon's brow lifted.

"Well," Trinon turned back to look down at her, "Mota began the prodding, and, well."

"Explain yourselves."

"We wanted to see if he could climb the monolith." Trinon's tongue slipped out between his lips and Chardon reached up to grab it with the intention of harm. Trinon was faster bobbing sideways to the right.

"He's not a man beast." Chardon chided him.

"Close enough," a new voice replied from behind Trinon.

Mota came up to them with Chardon's son, Farin, in tow. He was only an inch or two taller than Trinon even though he was much older. They were resembling their father more as the years went on. Mota set Farin down and brushed some loose dirt off the sides of his robes before letting him go to his mother.

Farin was tragically beautiful, which was one of the reasons why Chardon felt others wanted to pick on him. He had stark black hair with slight golden colored waves in it and murky green eyes. Instead of fingernails, he had shiny black talons sharper than any cutting weapon. His full pink mouth that he inherited from Chardon completed the exotic features.

"They dared me to climb the big stone!" Farin's small voice attempted yelling. "My claws just slid on it and couldn't grip!" Chardon saw his disappointed.

"Yes, well, next time they tease you, slice a piece of it off."

Trinon and Mota's posture went erect at such a suggestion. Mota raised a hand in protest.

"Let's not get all out of sorts over a little fun and games."

Chardon sighed. "We are leaving soon and I don't want any incidents."

"Trinon is going to accompany him, so you need not worry." Mota turned back towards the way he came. "I'll see you off when the time comes. I have to tend to the other little ones."

He walked away, and Chardon wondered how he got his personality. Neither of his parents were what one might call cheerful.

Chardon watched Modas, her personal bodyguard, wait in silence as she tended to a dirty Farin in the basin embedded in the chamber's floor. He didn't move an inch for the duration of the event and there was an expression on his face that Chardon did not like. How Modas felt towards Halfar was no secret. In her opinion that should not transfer to her child.

"Could you hand me a drying cloth?"

"As you wish."

Modas stepped further into the chamber, removed a cloth from its rack and handed it to Chardon. He never came any closer than required.

"Am I not worthy of your loyalty and protection any longer?"

"You will always have both."

"That's not why I asked, Modas." Chardon spat through gritted teeth.

"What is it you want from me?"

"Stop treating us like pariahs!"

"Understood"

Chardon slapped the wet cloth on the floor, startling both Farin and Modas, and turned to stare at Modas. Her eyes filled with tears.

"Does Modas not like Farin?" Farin asked softly, his eyes opened to their full extent.

Modas' in turn grew wide with shock and obvious shame.

"I do like Farin, very much."

Farin, stark naked and not yet fully dry, smiled sweetly.

"I'll go prepare for the trip to Azrom," he said to Chardon as he left.

In the hallway, Modas strode hurriedly towards the exit. At the end of the corridor he stopped, took a deep shaky breath and smashed his fist against the wall. His head hung down in despair. This was not how he envisioned Chardon's life. As her bodyguard, he should have prevented all that transpired from happening.

Raising his head, he looked up at the weak sun mocking him from above. If it were not for Halfar and his childish tantrum they would still be on their home world. And Chardon would be safe. He would have got- ten rid of Sestis easy enough in the beginning, before she had a foothold within the council.

Tiny laughter caught his ear and he cringed with pain. His little ones were playing in the fields further out and adjusting his vision saw Jaron, his mate and Chardon's cousin, playing with them. He loved her, he did. But, he wondered if things could have been different if he was not for- bidden from who he wanted initially. Would it have made me happy?

Modas straightened his posture and continued towards the council room for briefing regarding their departure. The selection of people the council chose to accompany Chardon was not to his liking.

His son, Trinon, was acceptable. Talas and Kelin he could do without. He had to deal with it because when it came to strategy Talas had no equal and he didn't go anywhere without Kelin. Even more amazing was Jaron and Talas combining their talents lately. Modas sighed heavily. He had hoped to at least minimize Chardon's interactions with Halfar, mate or not.

To read more please purchase

Seeds of Conviction

Core: Book Two

from your favorite online retailer

ABOUT THE AUTHOR

Maquel A. Jacob began her passion for the written word at the age of seven, reading everything she could get her hands on, including encyclopedias and the thesaurus. At twelve, she had her first encounter with a Stephen King novel and was hooked. She became inspired to write her own brand of fiction. Combining multiple genres is her way of keeping things interesting.

She is also a huge Anime fan, loves a great bottle of wine and rocks out to heavy metal music. Green and lush Oregon is where she currently resides spinning imaginary worlds in her head and daydreaming.

For updates, FREE short stories, Newsletters
...and more
Visit: www.maquelajacob.com

Like Maquel A. Jacob on Facebook
Follow on Twitter @Rachel_Robinso
Also find her on Goodreads

www.ingramcontent.com/pod-product-compliance
Lightning Source LLC
Chambersburg PA
CBHW021011120726
47905CB00009B/2956